A Small Wonder

To Live and Die in the Most Dangerous City in America!

By: Kevin Black

STREET KNOWLEDGE PUBLISHING

Published by: Street Knowledge Publishing

Street Knowledge Publishing
P.O. Box 345
Wilmington, DE 19899

Copyright date: 2016
ISBN: 978-1-944151-32-4
A Small Wonder by Kevin Black
Edited by Navimjan Services LLC
Cover design by 31 Minds
Formatted by Krystol Diggs
Typed from handwriting to text by Vanessa Cooper

www.streetknowledgepublishing.com

Printed in Canada

Acknowledgements

All Praises are due to Allah and Allah alone, the Most Gracious, the Most Merciful. May Peace and Blessings be on the Prophet Muhammad and his household.

I would like to thank my mother for bringing me into this world and raising me along with my Grandmother; to become the man I am today. To my children, know that Dad has your back through it all. To my wonderful aunts, uncles, brothers, sisters, cousins, nieces, nephews and friends; I love all of you. To my chosen few comrades, silence is our weapon. Death before dishonor. Omerta.

I would also like to thank Joe Joe and the Street Knowledge Publishing for giving me a chance to showcase my talents.

Finally, I would like to thank my wife who has held me down throughout the most troubling times of my life. You never withered during the storm. Your love, loyalty and commitment to me are unparalleled. I owe you a lifetime of reciprocation. I love you with all of my heart.

Dedications

In memory of Quinton Dorsey, Domenico "Coco" Melton, Maurice "Moe Good" Goodman, and Artega "Artie" Green. Four of the realest men I've ever met.

And to all the standup honorable men and women locked down in the American Prison system; stay strong, stay fighting, never give up. Know that as long as I have air in my lungs, I will be your support system. Salute.

Chapter 1

Damn, I can't believe this shit is finally over. After twelve long years, I will be walking out these doors tomorrow, Insha Allah. Being in prison so long has made me a better man, but also a better criminal. This is the dilemma I am faced with going out into the free world. On one hand, I am a practicing "Deenin" Muslim who values family, who wants to get married and has strong morals and principles. On the other hand, the Shaytan is whispering to me to get money, press all the hot dudes and suckers, and get revenge for the deaths of my best friends who were murdered while I did this bid. I want to do the right thing, Walahi, I do. My grandma has hopes of me coming out there and being productive after all these years away. I can't let Nana down or my children. But, fuck that, I gots to get mines! Shaytan is a muthafucka!

"Devon Baker!...Baker!" Yells the fat white C-O snapping me out of my thoughts.

I walk over to the C-O's office, "What's up Callahan?"

"Here, you have to do your Merry-Go-Round."

I don't know why they make every inmate, before they go home, take a piece of paper around to the counselor, the infirmary, kitchen, school, chaplain, supervisor of the inmate's job, and the Warden to sign. *I should go around and cuss all these racist cracka's out. Starting with that fat ass Callahan.*

"Thanks, Callahan, Did they call the ten minute move yet?" I ask his fat ass instead.

5

"No." He replies and walks back to his desk.

You got that, cracka, I say to myself. Most of these C-Os don't have much of a life living up in the mountains. No entertainment and the only pussy they get is from an old busted looking white wife who is probably their own sister.

*****

Later on. . .12:01 p.m.:

"Yeah Champ, don't forget me when you get out there." My man Husain from Philly felt the need to say.

"Ahki, I keep telling you I ain't one of them other niggas who left out here and forgot all the good dudes in jail."

So many guys that I have walked miles around the rec yard with and broke bread with have went home and never wrote a letter, sent money, or books to me like they promised. I will never forget all the good men that I had the good fortune to bond with throughout my incarceration.

"What do they have in the chow hall?" Husain asks me.

"Man, I think burger and fries. I'm just trying to get the Warden to sign this Merry-Go-Round," I state.

The line for lunch is way around the corner and it's moving slow. I am praying that this nigga Husain don't ask me about that stupid ass Philadelphia Eagles sign again. I am a diehard Cowboys fan so he knows I hate the Eagles like little altar boys hate Catholic Priests.

Husain started it up on cue, "And don't forget to get my Eagles sign designed so you can hold it up at the Eagles vs. Cowgirls game either."

"I got you but I'm gonna get my man to hold it."

"Nah, you got to do it," he says, smiling.

"Yea, aight," I say reluctantly.

*****

Later on that night. . .6:50 p.m.:

I'm in the rec yard kicking it with some of the good dudes for the last time. Some of them are never going home and I gots to represent for them out in the free world. With pen and pad, I am writing everyone's requests and needs down; I aim to come

6

through for my comrades.

"You want some boxing magazines and a few dollars, right Sloan?" I ask my homie Sloan from Southwest Philly.

He used to spar with B-Hopkins back in the day up in Grateford prison. He still thinks he is nice.

"Yeah, get The Ring magazine D.B." Sloan says while pivoting on his toes throwing jabs as he shadow boxes.

Little Marty from Germantown whispers in my ear, "Just send me five grams of that dope up here, Salaam." He calls me by my Muslim name.

"Got you."

"Hey Shay! Holla at me!" I yell over to Marshay from 60th Street, West Philly.

Shay is as slick as they come. He's over in the corner telling the young boahs his war stories.

"Nadir, what you want me to do?" I ask my man Nadir from North Philly.

"Come on, Salaam, I want you to just stay out until I get out." Nadir says to me sincerely. And I know he is depending on me to be there when he touches down in three years.

"Nadir, Insha Allah, I'm gonna be there waiting on you to take you to King of Prussia for shopping," I smile at my partner.

"Hey, Pugs, what do you need me to handle for you?" D.B. asks his longtime friend Ricky "Pugs" Mallory from West Philly, who is booked because a vicious rat couldn't keep it gangsta when them slugs hit him.

"D.B., get that nigga to do the right thing and sign the affidavit so me, Hakim and them can get back in court." Pug says.

"I got you. And if he don't act right, you will read about it, Walahi!" D.B. tells his comrade.

"What you want, Light?" I ask Light from Bronx, NY.

Light is a tall light-skinned brother that is a cold freak.

"Get me a subscription to Hip Hop Weekly and find a bitch with at least a 40-inch ass and take a tape measure and wrap it around her titties, pussy and between her ass cheeks."

Everybody burst out laughing.

"Light, you a vicious freak boah," Little Marty says.

Then Light crazy ass puts me on front street when he says, "Shit, D.B. says he going out there to eat bitches assholes."

Damn, D.B., you gonna get all the bitches doing that. And make sure you put a strawberry in there and eat it out." My man Stacy, from East St. Louis says.

I just shake my head laughing at him. "You bogus Stacy!" I say using his East St. Louis slang.

I then ask Stacy what he wants me to do for him when I get out. Stacy is a bigger Cowboys fan than me, so I wasn't surprised when he asked me to go to a Cowboys game in Dallas and flick it up for him. For the next hour, I spend my time writing names, inmate numbers, and requests from about thirty good dudes. I'm going to represent for my niggas, Walahi!

*****

Back on the unit...9:00 p.m. (30 minutes before lockdown):

I gots to go holla at my boah Black from South Carolina. See, Black has been my venting bag and voice of reasoning for two years straight. I told him my entire life's story; the good and the bad. He knows how I feel about my kids' mothers. He knows I am going out there to do my thing in those streets. He knows how hard I fight with the inner NAS (inner self) to want to do the right things in life. He never judges me, no matter what. He does think I'm crazy by some of the things I tell him I'm going to do out there. Some stuff ain't believable in this day and age, but I'm a real nigga and real niggas do real things.

"Black, what's up with the what's up?" I greet him when I walk in his cell after knocking.

"Nuffin' much, D.B., tomorrow is your day to shine, huh?"

"You better know it," I respond sitting down on the toilet seat as he sits on his bed.

"D.B., don't go out there and fuck none of your baby-moms and give them the satisfaction."

He is totally right because they jive; they did me dirty during my bid.

"Do I look like a sucka, Black?"

"Yeah," he laughs.

"Nah, Black. I am going to take your advice when you told me to treat them good and respectful but kill them with being successful." I shoot Black's words back at him.

"D.B., remember our theme song, "All I wanna be, All I wanna be, All I wanna be is successful." Black sings the tunes of Drake's hit, 'Successful'.

I used to listen to Drake's song every night while I lay on my bunk in my cell, plotting and calculating all my moves like a chess master.

"Black, I got you when I get out. I will see you tomorrow before I roll out. I got to go holla at my homie Jay real quick." I tell Black, as I walk out of his cell.

As I am walking to Jay's cell, I look around at the masses of men sitting around watching T.V. All are mostly Black and Hispanics. It is probably ten white guys on the unit out of 120 inmates. Black people are only thirteen percent of America's population, but we make up majority of America's prison population. *I got to make a change*, I tell myself. My homeboy Jackie Jackson a.k.a., Jay from Delaware is at the microwave fixing a mac and soup as I walk up.

"Yiz-oh, Cannon!" Jay greets me.

"What's the deal, playa?" I respond back.

"You outta here tomorrow, you understand me?"

"Yeah, it's my turn, finally," I say.

"Take your time out there. Shit ain't how it used to be. You been gone twelve years and niggas is grimy and they have no loyalty." Jay tells me this while cutting up his summer sausage.

"Homeboy, them niggas ain't ready for me, straight up". I state seriously.

Jay says something next that saddens me, "Remember what happened to your man, Mark Golden when them bitches set him up to get robbed. He was getting all those bricks from the Mexican papi and he got blinded by those dollar signs. Then, BOOM. . .them wolves got on his line and used them dumb ass bitches to jam him."

My man Mark Golden, a.k.a., Markie Gold was tearing the city up. No, fuck that, he was tearing the East Coast up. He had a Mexican plug that was flooding him with 150-200 kilos of cocaine per week. He had the cars, the clothes, the jewelry, the bitches, the money and the fame. The nigga had some of the baddest bitches all over the country, but he had a weakness, this no-good whore named Jeanette. He was fucking this bitch for eleven years but she crossed him for that bread...then she herself got double-crossed. The same niggas who killed my man killed her and her girl.

I told Jay straight-faced, "I ain't my man Markie Gold."

"I hear you, Cannon. But, I know the City of Wilmington has been ranked the most dangerous city in America by News Week Magazine. It's no longer the Small Wonder. It is the murder capital and them young niggas ain't bullshit'n," Jay says as he looks me in the eyes.

"Them young niggas ain't got enough experience to fuck with me." I tell Jay without breaking eye contact.

"Talk that shit, Cannon."

*****

After lockdown in the cell . . .11:17p.m.:

My cellie Yahya (John Dillard) and I have just finished offering the Isha Salah (Night Prayer) and now we are kicking it for the last time. The federal judge gave Yahya forty years on his first offense. He is the quietest, most humble brother I know. You can't even tell he got forty years.

"Salaam, go out there and find you a nice Muslim wife, Akhi."

"I want to, Yahya, for real."

"You got to cling to the Masjid and be around the brothers who are deening."

"Damn, all my friends are Muslim, but ain't hardly none of them are full-time deening. I got a few, like Malik (Mike Winters) and Shareef (Shawn Truitt) that stay in the Masjid."

"Well, you should cling to them then," Yahya says humbly.

"I know Yah, but I need to get this money so I can start these businesses I have in mind," I say more to convince myself instead of Yahya.

"Look, Slim ere' body who tried to go out there bojangling

10

in the streets either go back to prison or die." Yahya done went Washington, D.C. on me.

"I am going to go hard for one year on until I get five million in cash. I will stop at whichever comes first."

"Salaam, I love you for the sake of Allah and like a blood brother. I want you to be safe out there."

"Just make dua for me, Yah."

"Insha'Allah. As-Salaamu-Alaikum, Champ."

"Walaikum As-Salaam, Yah."

I close my eyes, but, sleep doesn't come. I got big dreams like my man Meek Millz spit.

*****

The next morning. . .Release Day. . .7:30 a.m.:

"Inmate Devon Baker, report to R&D".

That's the call I've been waiting on for twelve long years and one month. It's my time to shine. I got all my pictures and paperwork in a grey net bag, flung over my shoulder and about thirty of my closest comrades are walking me to R&D. Yahya, Husain, Nadir, Black, Jay, Light, Lil Marty, Shay, Sloan, Twin (NJ), Stacy, Samir, XO (Bronx), R-Mel (NY), Fat Will (Norristown), Tay (B-more), Dirty (B-More), Dee-Bo (Boston), Freaky, Saddiq, Mexican Cano, Dominican Christian, Shawn Alexander, Tike (Camden), Young Boah Party, Italian Lenny, Chinese Ocean, Big Roscoe (DC), Q (Connecticut), and Douglas Denson (Rhode Island). The whole crew is here to walk a stand up nigga to the door. Hard-core killers and gangbangers, cold men, are literally in tears. A real nigga like me is even crying like a bitch at a Michael Jackson concert. Some of these guys will not be able to drive a car or walk down the street again until they are in their 60s-90s. I am going to hold my niggas down like nobody ever did who left the feds.

"As soon as I get out these doors I am going to send each of you $50 a piece just to show you I ain't faking. Then once I get out and settled in, I will be hitting you'll with more money." I hug all my niggas and tell them to hold their heads up. They wish me well as I walk through the doors of R&D.

My peoples sent me a blue Polo sweat suit and a pair of blue and white Jordan 5s to wear home. It feels so good putting on street clothes after years of wearing khakis. The C-O at the desk gives me my bus ticket and twenty-five dollars of travel money after I sign my release papers. I told my counselor that I was catching the bus home so I could get more travel time. However, my squad is supposed to be picking me up at the bus station.

"Ok, Mr. Baker, let's go so that I can take you to the bus station," C-O Roberts says as he leads the way through a series of security doors.

Butterflies are tearing my stomach up. I am actually nervous that I'm leaving a hell that I've been in for twelve years to face an unknown future. Walking outside into the prison parking lot felt incredible! I can imagine how our slave ancestors felt once Harriet Tubman led them to free land. *Give us us free!*

Once C-O Roberts drops me off at the bus station, it really hits me...that I am a free man. I search around looking for my ride because the bus is loading up about to depart. I am debating whether I should get on this bus or wait for my crew. I have to be in the halfway house by 12:15 a.m. and I can't be late.

"Niggas are always late," I say quietly to myself. As I am about to board the bus despondently, I hear Young Jeezy and Jay-Z song 'As Real as It Gets,' banging from my cousin's silver Cadillac Escalade. All I see is my other cousin's, Vance Baker's, big ass lips through the windshield. Once they pull over and park, my crew emerges from the truck as I diddy-bop over to them with a big ass grin on my face.

As they welcome me home with hugs and pounds, I rap to Jeezy's verse, "I ain't dead or in jail, I can't complain!"

Chapter 2

We're cruising down the highway as I'm chopping it up with my squad listening to them tell me all that I missed over the years and how the "family" business is doing. I am astonished by what I hear. A lot of money is definitely being made, but their system and security is flawed. I'm surprised that the Feds haven't swopped down yet, or even worse, the wolves haven't attacked. I definitely have to get this shit airtight, for real.

Listening to all this bullshit got me so caught up, I forgot to introduce you to the squad. . .niggas who I'd die for. My pops, Samuel Bowman is behind the wheel, pushing the luxury truck on an eight-hour drive to Delaware. This guy loves to drive; he should have been a truck driver. In the passenger seat, sits my little cousin Darnell Lyons. He is high as a kite off the O.G. Kush and he's rolling another blunt right now. *Damn, I got a contact!* He is a long-legged, dread, slim built, about 6-foot-2. Sitting next to me is my other cousin Vance Baker. He thinks he's God's gift to women. He stands about 6-foot-2 skinnier than J.J. off of Good Times and he has 360 degree waves, well, 320 degrees. He needs to get his brush game up. We are all first cousins. Our parents are siblings. The bloodline is intact. Lastly, we got my brother from a different mother; my partner in crime. A nigga who been there for me since day one. My man, William Holiday, but we call him "Umar"; a tall skinny dude who resembles Snoop Dog. He is the only nigga in Wilmington still rocking braids. *Nigga, A.I. been left the Sixers.*

"Damn Umar, blow that smoke out the window." I complain, while having a coughing fit.

"Nigga, I see you still got baby lungs. Remember I smoked you under the table back in the day? We were playing NBA Live and you nodded off with the blunt in your mouth." Umar is laughing and coughing as he replays the story.

"Nigga, what about the time I mixed the Hawaiian, the Chocolate Thai, The Dominican, and the Hash together? You fell asleep driving on I-95 and I had to grab the wheel!"

I was the smoke out King back in the day. Vanny B. chimed in next with a nostalgic memory that we all had to remember....

"Remember my first day home after doing the three years? Y'all let me hit the Purple Haze and the Remy. I was so buckled (high), that y'all went into AppleTree Jamaican restaurant and left me in the car."

"Yeah Nigga." I laughed, "You had one leg hanging out the car door, the car light was on, and you still had your seat belt on."

"That was the night we had the bitches Mimi, Monique, and Lyric with us," my cousin Darnell says.

Vanny B. turns serious, "My baby Lyric wasn't no bitch cuz. RIP Lyric. That was my baby," Vanny B. whispers.

Lyric was his son's mother who was struck by a stray bullet intended for the guy who was gunned down right next to her.

To live and die in the city of Wilmington....

We ride the rest of the way laughing and joking. I'm telling prison stories while they are telling me street stories. I also explain to them how we can get more money and expand into other cities, but first, we have to tighten our system and security up. I'm not trying to be sitting up in a federal pen because of someone else's mistakes. I already did a bid.

We stop in Philly so that they can take me shopping for clothes. South Street is lit up. There are way more clothing boutiques now on South Street than there were before. Bitches are everywhere! Each of my crew gives me a big ass Chester Knot. We used to call big wads of money "Chester Knots" because back in the day if you went up in William Penn

Projects, in Chester, PA, the hustlers would have big wads of money on them. In total, I had about $4000 to spend on clothes, well actually $2500 because I got to send my niggas in jail $50 a piece like I promised. My word means everything to me.

I have a list of what types of jeans are in style. A dude named Torry from Newark, NJ put me on the game before I left prison. So here I am in this chic boutique trying to piece it together, but I'm clueless. I've always been a fly dresser, but it's a new era. Shit, it's tighter with that Euro-cut.

"Do you need any help?" The pretty dark-skinned girl asks me.

"Yeah, I could use a woman's touch," I say to her, flashing my million-dollar smile.

All the woman who used to come visit me fell in love with my perfectly even white teeth.

"You just came home didn't you?" she bluntly asks.

"Yeah, how did you know?"

"Because, you have a glow and your teeth are perfect and your lips aren't all black like these niggas out here." She states.

I blush and smile again while I pull out the list of jeans and give it to her. "Do you have these jeans?" I ask.

Torry wrote down the names of all the top brands out at the time. True Religion, 7 for Mankind, Rock & Republic, Joe, Hudson, Red Monkey, Monarchy, D&G, Diesel, etc.,

"We got True's, 7's, Rock & Republic and Monarchy. I got you. What size you wear?" She is trying to get this sell for sure.

"I wear 36/32." I sit back and let her work her magic.

"Here, try this cute designer thermal on." She says handing it to me.

I take off my Polo sweatshirt in the middle of the store to try on the thermal. Underneath I have a tank-top on.

Shorty takes one look at twelve years of hard work and screams, "God Damn, you look like an action figure! Can I touch your arms?"

She is dead serious too. I worked out hard for twelve years so I could have this effect on women. After homegirl visually rapes me and gets her lust on, I pay for my clothes and bounce.

My family is having a "welcome home" dinner for me at my Grandma's and I can't wait to eat some real food. I'm snapping pictures with a disposable camera I grabbed from CVS; got to send my niggas pics of my first day out.

As we are walking back to the truck my cousin Darnell says, "Ain't that the porn bitch Pinky right there?" Pinky! My first thought is, *my niggas in jail would go crazy for some real Pinky pics starring me.* I follow her into Dr. Denim clothes store.

"Hey Pinky! Let me holla at you." I say, like I really know the stanking whore.

"Hi, what's up?" She says to me.

"Do you know you are a legend up in the federal jails?"

She is giving me the same look as the girl I just left at the clothing boutique, "I am?"

I ask her can I take some pictures of her so I can send to my niggas. I toss the camera to my cousin Darnell and Pinky and I flick it up. I'm grabbing her ass; pointing at it for my nigga Light. He loves Pinky. After we finish, I thank her and she hands me a flyer to the party she is hosting then I'm out!

*****

Later than night...7:30 p.m.:

We ride past the "Welcome to Delaware" sign on I-95 in Claymont, DE, on my way to my grandma's house.

"Umar, let me see your cell phone real quick." I say to my man.

I don't know how to work this new tech shit. I got a lot to learn. I call a buddy of mines named Sharnay. She kept a nigga with flicks and visits during my bid. She lives in Claymont, so I tell my pops to get off at the Naamans Road exit. We pull up to her condo and I tell my crew that I will be back in five minutes. I'm just going up here to give her a hug and thank her for ridin' for a nigga. However, Sharnay has other plans. I knock on the door only to hear Sharnay's sweet voice, "Come in."

I come in alright, to scented candles, R. Kelly's '12 Play' pumping on the stereo and Sharnay laying on the couch with some "fuck me" lingerie on. *Oh my God! She is phat as shit.* A chocolate bunny with an ass like Buffie the Body.

16

I tell her, "I can't stay. My peoples waiting on me outside."
"They can wait." She purrs.

She leaps off the couch and I tongue her down as I grab that big ass of hers with both hands. She's trying to unbuckle my belt as she massages my dick to its full extension. I attempt to do something that is as difficult as trying to get the Pope to sniff some coke – I try to back away from this horny lioness.

"You look so goooood, Devon. Damn, you got my pussy wet." She says seductively.

My game plan coming out of prison is to get my bank roll up before I start fucking with these hoes. *Stick to the plan D.B.,* I tell myself.

I back up towards the door and say, "My family made dinner for me and I am late. I gotta roll."

"Come on, just five minutes," she begs.

"I'm home now. I got you. I'm gonna beat that pussy up on my first home pass." I lie to her.

The first woman I stick this prize wood in is going to be my Muslim wife. Allahu Akbar! If I manage to escape out there still a born again virgin. I thank her and promise to call her later.

As soon as I get back in the truck, Vanny B. asks, "What that pussy felt like?"

Everybody is looking at me cheesing, but I shock the shit out of them when I relay what happened upstairs.

"How the fuck you don't want no pussy after twelve years, my nigga?" My cousin Darnell loudly asks.

I tell my Pops to cut the radio down before I drop this precious jewel on them, "You can't get no money chasing bitches, but, if you chase the money and acquire it, then you will get all the bitches chasing you."

Chapter 3

It's been twelve years and one month since I walked through the doors of my Nana's house. The house seems so small. All of my family and close friends are there to welcome me home.

Boy, did they set it out for a playa on the food tip. My mom, aunts, and Nana made lamb chops, macaroni and cheese, fried cabbage, baked chicken wings, curry goat, rice and peas, potato salad, banana pudding, and a bangin' ass cake. We are having a ball. *I really miss my family.* Everyone is vying for my attention. I go outside and flick it with my children and friends. My sons, Devon Jr. and Deverick dwarf me. They both stand over six feet tall.

"Come on over and take a picture with me Devona," I call out to my daughter who is staring at me from a distance.

"No, I'm okay." She meekly says.

My daughter has always been withdrawn from me during all of our visits in prison. She has some type of resentment towards me. But I am determined to be a father to my children by spending quality time with them and not just with material things.

"Girl, get over here and show your dad some love." Her mother Tisha spat. Tisha keeps giving me googly eyes, but she must have thought I forgot what she did while I was on lock down.

"Kill them with success." I can hear my boy Black saying in my head.

18

I take more flicks with my young boahs Skully and Bay-Bay. I've raised these two niggas since I gave them their first package to sell when they were thirteen years old. Now, they are grown men with big beards and prostration markers on their foreheads. My homegirls Valerie, Marie, and Tijuana Pennewell jump all in the picture too.

"Hold up, hold up, where's Brick at?" I ask out loud. "We can't take a Westside flick without Brick. Go get him Lil' Devon." I tell my son.

Brick is my other partner in crime. He did thirteen in the Feds and just came home two years ago.

After everyone goes home, it's just my grandma, my mom, my boy Funk, and I sitting in my grandmom's kitchen. It's 11:15 p.m. and Funk is dropping me off at the Plummer Center Halfway House.

My Nana starts one of her lectures, "Devon, you have been gone for a long time. I wish your grandpa was alive to see you free again. I pray that you never have to go back to that place again as long as I am alive."

"I'm not, Nana."

"Leave them streets alone. People are getting killed every day. And stay away from that 5th Street."

How the hell can I stay away from 5th Street? I think to myself.

Nana continues on, "Promise child that you are going to find you a good church gal and settle down and get married before I go to be with your grandpa."

"Yes, Nana, I plan on getting married but it will not be to a church girl," I laugh.

"He is Muslim, Mom." My mom tells Nana.

"Mom, I'm gonna give you about five more grand kids," I say, as I hug my mother.

I kiss my Nana good bye and walk my mom to her car.

"Funk, I got to be at the Plummer House by 12:15 a.m., come on, take me to Western Union real quick." I say to him as we ride down Lancaster Ave.

I got to represent my niggas behind the wall.

*****

I've been at the halfway house for about a week now. Sucker ass C-O Carter is trying to get me sent back to the Feds. He hating because the whole city is coming through showing me a lot of love. Niggas and chicks I ain't heard from in twelve years are coming through dropping off clothes, cosmetics and money. Young broads, 21-22 years old, who I don't even know are stopping by to see me.

Niggas from all sides of town are passing off a few dollars. I accept it with a smile, but I see right through these sucka ass niggas. They know it is inevitable that I am going to turn the city on fire, so they think by looking out for me now that I will put them on when them birds come through. Or, that I will not put the press on them. I feel like you got to press all suckers and rats. Put the squeeze on the suckers early because they have the potential to tell on a real nigga later on. That's what Lil' Brucie told me. Suckers told on him and now he got a life sentence.

My cousins Darnell and Darius have a restaurant and lounge called the "Regal" and they let me "work" there so I can get out the halfway house daily. The joint be jumping, especially on Thursday, Friday, and Saturday nights for happy hour and beyond. It's the place to be in Wilmington. During the day, the working class professionals like judges, lawyers, doctors, bank managers, and government workers enjoy the meals or the bar. Then at night, all the hood celebrities come out in their finest gear. So, you know a nigga is feeling the setup.

*****

Tuesday at the Regal 1:12 p.m.:

I am at "work" kickin it with my boys Skully and Bay-Bay at the window table that has become my unofficial office. Skully is bragging about all the bitches he fucked.

"I fucked the bitch Sharnay all in her ass."

I spit the apple juice I was drinking. "You talkin bout my bitch, Sharnay?" I said in shock.

"Yeah nigga and she said 'you act just like D.B.,' I told her I know because he's like my pops." Skully and Bay-Bay are laughing like shit funny.

"I'm glad I didn't fuck that bitch because she don't deserve this dick." I gladly boasted.

Bay-Bay asked me why I ain't want no pussy yet. They can't believe I been home one month and still didn't fuck a bitch yet.

I tell them straight up, "Look at me. My waves spinnin', my skin is glowing, my teeth are perfect, and my body is ripped up. So why should I just give any ol' broad all this?" I say, waving my hand up and down my body. I continue on, "They not gonna get the chance to suck my glow away. Plus, I ain't trustin' none of these hoes that easy so they can set me up like they did Markie Gold."

"I know you wish you was home when Markie Gold was getting all that money." Skully says to me.

"Damn right! I would've made sure my nigga was straight. Niggas would've never tried that bullshit had I been home."

"When are we going to get some shit?" Bay-Bay asks me. Skully has hope in his eyes.

"I don't know. I only been home one month."

"Shit, your peoples Paul Baker got all the coke and weed. Why don't you holla at them?" Skully is pressing me. As soon as I was about to answer his thirsty ass, my phone rings. "Hello." I answer. It's my other partner in crime, Quincy Dorsett, calling from Smyrna State Prison.

"D.B., As-Salaamu-Alaikum."

"Walaikum As-Salaam." I return the greeting.

"Thanks for the $200 you sent me and the magazines."

"Come on man, that ain't nothing."

"Yeah...but you just came home and you got to get yourself together first."

"Q, if I got it, you got it." I say confirming my loyalty to him.

"What it feel like to be home?" He asks me.

"It feels great! The bitches are sweating me to smash, but I ain't hit nothing yet."

"That's right. Get your money right first. Fuck them hoes." That's why I love this dude. He thinks just like me. "Yo, when do you come home?"

"In about four months. And it's on, too!" He emphatically states.

"I'll be ready by then. I got you."

"Hey D.B., it's about to be count time so let me go. I'll hit you next week, Insha'Allah."

"Ok, do that. Tell Lil' Dave Tolbert and Curt Demby I said what up."

"Ok, As-Salaamu Alaikum."

"Walaikum As-Salaam."

As soon as I hang up, Skully asks "When does Q. get out?" I tell him, "In four months."

"It's going to be on then. The whole squad is going to be out together." he says, all animated and shit.

"Yeah, it's going to be our turn to shine. Are you niggas ready or not?" I'm just testing them by asking this question.

Bay-Bay puts his iPhone down and says, "What? Are we ready? Damn straight."

"Man, them Eastside niggas are winning right now. Beeks and Ranji. But we gonna show them how it's done." Skully says with hunger in his eyes.

"We will see, we will see." I nod my head, approvingly.

*****

Later on that week at the Regal. . .12:30 p.m.:

I just finished up writing a few letters to my never forgotten homies in prison. I hope my man Steven Leath a.k.a. S.L. smiles when he gets the flicks I sent him. I sent Husain, Black, Yahya, Meatball and Butter $150 a piece earlier today, so they should be good. I'll shoot to Street Knowledge Book Center later so I can send Sloan them boxing magazines he wants. I got to represent for my niggas.

"Hey D.B.!" Funk's wife, Chevell, comes in screaming my name at the top of her lungs.

"What's up, Vell?" I say, as I walk over to her and her friend she has accompanying her.

"Are you treating us to lunch?" She asks.

"You know I got you. Hi, how are you doing?" I flash the

million dollar smile on Chevell's friend as I speak.

"I'm fine and you?" She smiles back.

"Oh, my bad, Devon, this is my homegirl Jasmine. Jasmine, this is my brother Devon."

We all enjoyed our lunch while we conversed about an array of topics. During the entire conversation I notice Jasmine looking at me like I was sirloin steak and she was a hungry tigress. It's the same look that I see most women giving me. I walk Chevell and her friend to their car and say my goodbyes. No sooner than fifteen minutes later, Chevell calls from her work phone.

"D.B., my girl Jasmine asks can she have your number?"

"Oh yeah?" *I'm not surprised*, I think to myself.

"What you want me to tell her?"

"Go ahead and give her my number Vell."

These chicks are on a nigga like a tailor-made suit. I want to see how they act when this star turns into a super star.

Chapter 4

Friday at the Regal. . .9:10 a.m.:

I am sitting at my table bustin it up with my mans Brick, Umar, and lil' cousin Deen Baker. Who goes by the name D.B. as well. Where they do it at, he represents the name though. We are trying to figure out who came around the way dumping in broad day light and hit Burley and X. Both of them are Lil' Devon's boys, so I banned Lil' Devon from the Westside until shit calms down.

"Hey, come here for a second cuz." My cousin Paul calls me from the back of the kitchen.

I get up and stroll to the back. "What up cuzzo?" I ask him.

He is standing there with some gay looking Spanish dude who is smiling at me.

"Cuz, this is my main man, Primo. Primo, this is my crazy cousin D.B. I used to tell you about."

"What's up? I heard a lot of good things about you." Primo says, while shaking my hand.

My cousin adds, "I told him you can move your ting like Tony Montana," he says in his accent.

"I mean, I'm alright, I guess." I say modestly.

"While you was locked up, Primo tried to throw me 500 Kilos, but I was like, Hell no! Coke is your ting and the weed is my 'ting'." My cousin lets that be known.

So this Mexican nigga comes right out and asks me, "So, what are you trying to do?"

"What do you mean?" I had to ask.

24

"How much coke can you handle?"

"Man, I don't know. I only been home one month."

My cousin Paul had the nerve to say I was scared. *Is he retarded? D.B. scared? Picture that!*

"Look, I will start you off with 30 kilos to see how you do." Primo says, but, he just doesn't realize how I am about to fuck the city up.

Primo promises that the driver will deliver the coke next Saturday, so I got about one week to get shit in order. He is frontin' me the birds at 28K a pop. Plus, I got to pay the driver 1K for each kilo he delivers. So, 30 kilos at 28K a piece comes to $840K, plus 30K for the driver. A total of $870K I owe Primo. I can get rid of the birds in the tristate area for $36K a piece and that's a deal.

Well...I can't move the shit because I've been out of the loop, but my squad can and they are ready to. I'll tell my squad to let them go for 36K and give me back $33.5K. So, I'm making $4500 off each brick and my team makes $2500 off of each one. Them niggas are chefs so they'll probably put their whip game down they can turn 1 kilo into a kilo and a half. My profit off my first flip will be $135K cash. *I'm back!*

*****

This week I have been busy trying to line everything up. This halfway house is in the way. I got to find Primo's two relatives somewhere to stay. They have to get the money when I am done. I might ask my homegirl Marie can they stay at her crib since she is half Spanish. Or they can stay at my brother's crib on Franklin Street in the Spanish part of town. Next, I got to find a place to hold all those birds. I'm going to pay someone $2500 to babysit the birds until all of them are finished. I am going to give them two P-89 handguns, a play station, DVD player, radio and I'll bring their food to them. I got to get burnout phones for me and each of my men. I know that the Feds tap phones at a high rate, but I sat in that cell and figured out how to beat them. For example, the phones I get for me and Umar are only to be used by me and him with one another.

Then, I will get two separate phones for use by my cousin Deen and I. So I will have about six phones. *Fuck that!* Now here is where I run into a small problem. I can't be naked out here. Gots to have that hammer close once that money starts rolling in. But I'm in the halfway house and I can't carry a gun. I need one of these youngins from around the way to be my shadow. Go wherever I go with that hammer. I gots to be able to trust the lil' nigga though. I had my eyes on a few youngins who I heard was murdering everything. I heard about the boah Littles. I like how the young nigga Cousin Gee be moving too. He got about five bodies under his belt. Skully had introduced me to this pretty boy named Allen who supposed to be the best kept secret. I'm going to holla at all three of them niggas.

I got everybody on point. Shit is airtight. I'm just waiting on the truck driver to come through Saturday. I'm at the Center watching my son Deverick's basketball practice.

"Come on Deverick, you have to hustle harder than that." I yell to my son in order to motivate him.

I am waiting on his mom Cheryl to come. I told her I needed to holla at her. Five minutes later, she comes strutting in the gym.

"Devvvvonnnn" she sings my name.

"What up, Cheryl?" I say. She speaks to our son before sitting down.

"Listen Cheryl, I don't trust too many people out here. I trust you. I'm about to turn it up a notch and get this money."

"But why though? It's not the same out here." She reminds me.

"I got a plan. I'll be in and out in a year." I got a vicious Mexican connect and he is about to hit me. It will be almost like Markie Gold."

"Do you see what happened to him?" She says almost in tears.

"My point exactly. That's why I wanted to holla at you. Once that G-5 and them birds start moving, bitches are gonna come from everywhere; and only because I will have money. I don't want no girlfriend or nothing, but I want someone I can hang out with sometimes. You know, go to a movie or dinner, shit like that. If I want to have sex, she will be my only sex partner. And, I will take care of all her bills, etc." I pause to let it sink into her head.

"So, are you saying you want me to be that woman?"

"Duh. You are the only girl that I trust."

"I don't want that lifestyle no more. I'm scared."

"I feel you." I admit to her.

"Plus, I don't got time to deal with all of your bitches or the ones that will come."

"Cheryl, I haven't even had sex yet since I been home."

"Stop lying boy." She says as she mushes my head.

"Walahi! I'm not thinking about no bitches. I'm about to get this paper."

"Umm Umph, Devon. . .I can't do it." She shakes her head no.

"Are you sure?" I ask one last time.

"Yeah." She replies as if she lost her best friend.

*****

Friday - Jummu'ah at Ar- Razak Masjid...1:41 p.m.:

"Anything I said that was beneficial and correct was from Allah (subhana wa ta' Ala) alone and anything that I said that was wrong, not in accordance with the Qur'an and Sunnah, was from me and the whispers of the Shaytan. May Allah forgive me. Yaaa Mukhalibal Qooloob, Othabit Qawbi 'Aladeenic. Iqamas-Salat."

After Jummu'ah, I stand outside the masjid talking to Malik, Shareef, Bay-Bay and York.

"What days are the classes on, Akhi?" I ask Malik.

"We got an Arabic class on Tuesdays after Magrib prayer. Thalatal-Usool is on Thursdays. And Aqidah Wasitiyah is on Saturdays after Ars Prayer."

"Insha'Allah I'll start coming to classes." I say, sincerely.

Malik pulls me to the side, "Salaam, you got to watch your Sahabas (companions). You got to come around the masjid more than Jummu'ah and a few prayers. You can't have one foot in the dunya (streets) and one foot in the religion. What

27

happens if you step on a banana peel?" He asks.

I contemplate all that he says.

All I can say is, "Make dua for me that I don't slip on that banana peel."

Chapter 5

One week later – At Vanny B's house:

I'm chillin with my four cousins, Paul, Darnell, his brother, Darius and Vanny B. They got the O.G. Kush in the air and are getting their drink on. We are discussing the next shipment; crunching numbers and trying to figure out who got to do what. Me and my squad ran through the thirty keys in five days. Primo texts me and says he is sending fifty joints next week. I made 135K, easy money. *It's on!* I'm laid back on the couch, listening to my cousin Darnell give us the price on his "ting", "The Chronic."

I got on a royal blue Versace hoodie, light colored Seven jeans, black Versace belt, and a pair of $800 Versace sneakers. Oh, it's only 11:05 a.m. This is how I am rollin now. I threw away all my Timberlands, Lebron's, and the regular average joe gear. I had to step my game up on these niggas out here. Only the flyest exclusive shit for me, like Louis Vuitton, Gucci, Versace, Giuseppe, Louboutin's (for Men), D&G, Balmain, Lanvin, etc.; every day, all day, and I wear that shit in the rain! I only wear Nikes to the gym.

"Primo said he found the lime green fluffy shit." My cousin Darnell tells us.

Darius must've been reading my mind. He asks, "How much he talking?"

"$600 a pizzy," answers Darnell. I quickly add up the numbers in my head; 600 a pound and we pay the driver $50 per pound. That's $650 and I let them go for $1000 each. We need to get on it because my man Big Dawg from Chester keeps asking can I get the A-Z. He said he can move about 300-400 pounds a week.

I tell cuz, "I'm going to grab 100 of them to see how it do."

"Ok cuddy, I see you doing big things." Darius says while giving me some dap.

"Shit, nigga just got rid of thirty bricks in a few days and he only been in the Plummer House one month." That's Darnell bragging about my hustle game.

"Cuddy, next time you get some shit, holla at me because I got some niggas who want some joints." Vanny B. puts in his bid, early.

"I got you, cuz." I tell him.

Paul gets Vanny B's, Darnell's, and Darius' order and adds his and mines with it.

"Ok, we getting 1100 pizzies. I need the change by Sunday so I can have it ready for the driver." Darnell informs us.

As we are walking out of Vanny B's crib, I see Jambo, Dumbs, Tommy Jr., and a few dudes sitting in the park across the street.

"As-Salaamu Alaikum." I salaam Dumbs and Jambo.

"Walaikum As Salaam". What up, Tommy Jr.?"

"You the man I'm trying to see, D.B." Tommy hollas back.

Jambo walks over to me, "What's up, Dev?"

"I'm chillin, Bo. Just glad to be home." I respond.

"I hear you got it, too. When you going to holla at me?" *He heard that shit kind of fast. I got to keep it a little more quiet.*

"Bo, look man, if we do something, you got to keep my name out of it because I don't want the Feds on my line."

"D.B., ain't I trustworthy?"

I look him straight in the face and say, "That was back in the day, but you be hanging with some funny niggas now."

"Who?"

"Man, you know who. Just keep them out of our mix."

So much has changed over the years. Niggas are tellin on their brothers and their best friends just to get out from doing time. Jambo asks for my phone number.

"Hit me next week and give Tommy Jr. my number, too." I tell him as I walk away.

A grey Maxima with a light tint pulls up and stops.

"Who is that?" Jambo asks.

"Just my peoples." I say, as I open the Maxima door and jump in. My youngin was on point the whole time I was in Vanny B's crib. Trained to go with their hammers on their laps.

It's clutch time.

*****

Meanwhile around the way. . .

Brick, Umar and Tims sit lounging around in Valerie's house.

"Yo, niggas is callin my horn like shit." Tims blurts out the blue after sitting his phone down.

"Yeah, everybody want some of that yola we had." Brick states.

"I sold eight babies (4.5 ounces) in about four hours. That shit was butter even after I took a half ounce out each one and sprinkled baking soda in the bag." Tims reveals his bake trick. By taking half an ounce out of each four and a half, and replacing it with half an ounce of baking soda, he gains four free ounces. And you don't even notice it.

"Shit, I whipped one brick into two joints and sold ounces for $700." Umar tells them like he is some legitimate salesman.

"Niggas bought that garbage?" Brick asks Umar.

"That shit wasn't garbage, cuz."

"I'm gonna need you to whip my shit up for me next time." Brick wants to see that $50K off a bird like Umar did.

"Pop! Pop! Pop!" The sound of the gunfire causes Tims and Umar to instinctly reach for their guns in their waistbands.

"Somebody banging that hammer outside." Tims says.

Minutes later, all of their phones are blowing up with calls.

*****

A few minutes earlier. . .

The park on 6th and Madison Street is jammed packed; Niggas hustling, playing ball, shooting dice, and just chillin. The broads are out there trying to look cute in search of a sponsor. School children are just getting out of school and they hang around aspiring to one day be in the mix once they get of age. Skully, Bay-Bay, MJ, Mase and them are sitting around Skully's black on black Camaro. He just copped the joint after he helped run the thirty bricks. He spends it as fast as he makes it.

"Hey Nika, come here with your phat butt." Skully yells out to Nika.

She is a young joint that stands about 5-foot-2, 125 pounds, small waist with a big ass bubble butt. She ain't the prettiest thing but she got a banging body.

"No boy. You so disrespectful." She rolls her eyes at Skully.

"Fuck you! You dirty bitch!"

"Fuck your mom!" She spits.

Why did she say that? Skully's mom passed away five years ago. She was his world. Everybody got quiet because they know he don't play them mom games.

"What you say, bitch?" *Smack!* He smacks the shit out of Nika.

"Motherfucker, I'm gonna get my brother to fuck you up!" She screams while running up 6th Street.

"Fuck your clown ass brother." He yells at her.

Two minutes later, Nika and her brother Jo-Jo walk up to Skully.

"What's up Skully?" Jo-Jo grits on Skully.

"What you want to be up nigga?" he spats as he squares up ready to knock him out.

Bay-Bay, Mase and them surround Jo-Jo. Jo-Jo peeps the move and whips out a silver revolver. Niggas back up ASAP. Skully just got shot last year and he ain't tryin to feel that hot shit again, so he grabs Jo-Jo's hand that has the gun. They both are trying their best to get that gun. They are punching each other with their free hand. Skully's eyes are pleading with his men for help.

"Yo, grab this nigga!" Skully screams.

Bay-Bay and Mase are too paranoid to try to get in the scuffle because bullets don't have names on them.

"As Salaamu-Alaikum Akh. I'm Muslim. I'm not going to shoot." Jo-Jo throws that out there.

Hearing this causes Skully to let his guard down because he honors the Islamic Brotherhood. He lets go of Jo-Jo.

"Every brother ain't a brother. Pop! Pop! Pop!" Jo-Jo bangs Skully three times in his leg and foot and then takes off running up the street.

"Shit, Bay! Drive me to the hospital!" Skully screams in pain.

*****

Later on at Christiana Hospital...6:10 p.m.:

I'm sitting in the hospital room with Skully, trying to get the details of what happened.

"So, you smack the man's sister and thought he wasn't going to do nothing about it?" I ask incredulously.

"Man, fuck that nigga." Skully says lividly.

"Is he Muslim for real because if he is, we can't kill him?"

I need to know because a Muslim killing another Muslim is automatic Hellfire.

"I don't see him at Jummu'ah." Skully says.

"I'll check on it. If he is not Muslim then we will make him an example so niggas know not to fuck with us."

"Solid, solid."

On my way back to the halfway house, I'm in the car with my youngins Littles, Cousin Gee and Allen.

"Big Homie, what are we going to do about the nigga Jo-Jo?" Cousin Gee asks me.

"Is he Muslim?" I ask.

"Fuck no! He fucks with my cousin Miranda and he was over there eating the pork chops my aunt made."

Allen says as he turns around from the front passenger seat.

"Oh yeah?" My mind is plotting now.

"He don't know I fucks with you, so I can line him up easy." Allen says.

"I know. That's why I keep you in the cut." I admit to him.

"So, what's the deal?" He asks, eager to bust his gun.

"Tell him you know where Skully live at and you don't like

the nigga because he fucked your BM. It's an alley next to Skully's old house by Gander Hill prison. You take him there like you two are going to squat in the alley waiting for Skully to come out then you cook that nut ass nigga." I break it down for him.

"Yeah, he will bite on that easy." Allen agrees.

"We got to do this while Skully is still in the hospital so he won't be a suspect." I explain.

"I'm on it. I will set it up in two days." Allen says.

*****

Two days later at my homegirl Dana's house. . .

Dana is my best female friend. She holds me down through it all. I've known her over twenty-five years and she ain't never change. We have a genuine platonic friendship. I got the keys to her house and her car. That's my peoples for real.

I'm on the phone with a bad young broad I met at TD Bank. Her name is Rhonda. She is 5-foot-11, 165 pounds, brown-skinned, long shapely legs and a nice ass. You can tell she works out vigorously at the gym because she doesn't have any fat on her. She has been trying to give me the pussy for two weeks now. But I'm on a mission.

"Devon, you did twelve years in jail and you been home a month and a half, and you still haven't slept with anybody yet? Are you gay or something?" She giggles.

Hold up, I know this bitch didn't disrespect the kid. Got to check her, "Listen to this, Rhonda, don't you ever in your life again, associate me with no faggot shit or no snitch shit. I'm the realest nigga you ever met in your life. I don't fuck around!" I checked her hard.

"Jesus, I was only kidding."

"Well don't play with a real nigga." I tell her.

"Ok, I'm sorry." She melts easily.

A nigga do wants some pussy fa sho, but I have spoiled myself looking at all them Straight Stuntin, Smooth King and Black magazines with all them bad ass chicks. I ain't fuckin nothing but magazine material.

I promised my daughter Devona that I'd pick her up from

34

school and take her shopping. Realizing the time, I slide into my blue patent leather Gucci sneakers and brown Gucci leather jacket, ready to bounce.

"Come on, Cousin Gee. Take me to pick up Devona."

Chapter 6

Later that night near Skully's old house. . .9:09 p.m.:
"That's it right there. The second house from the corner."
Allen points as he drives past the house.

"I'm gonna slump that nigga this time," Jo-Jo says aloud.

"I'm going to park two blocks away so that after we bang him, we can just walk to the car and go." Allen fills Jo-Jo in on the move.

Allen parks the car on a little short street and the three gunmen walk towards Skully's house.

"This the alleyway right here. Come on, Jo." Allen creeps in the alley followed by Jo-Jo.

They both have their hoodies pulled tight over their heads, guns out, ready to cut Skully down. Jo-Jo is squatting down in front of Allen holding a .40 Caliber cannon.

"Damn, we been out here forty-five minutes. Do you think he's gonna show?" Jo-Jo asks Allen.

"That nigga can't move around like that. He on crutches." Allen tries to keep Jo-Jo at bay.

"Fifteen more minutes then I'm out. We can come back tomorrow night." Jo-Jo tells Allen.

That was Allen's cue right there. Allen raises the 9mm Sig Saurer to the back of Jo-Jo's head and squeezes the trigger twice. Jo-Jo head explodes open like a watermelon as he falls face first to the ground. Allen snatches Jo-Jo's gun from his hand and steps over him on his way out the alley.

*****

Next week at a warehouse in New Castle...2:22 p.m.:

We just finished unloading. There are forty-four boxes with twenty-five pounds of weed inside. And another four boxes with fifty keys of cocaine inside. Only a select few of the squad partakes in this sensitive part of the operation. My cousins, Darnell and Darius are here and my pops too with Umar, Rocky, Pooba, and myself. We got to break everything down and distribute what and to who. Then, my pops, Rocky, Pooba, and Umar take the stuff to the stash spots.

"Primo says he is going down to Mexico to holla at El Chapo's third in command. He says they got something big in the making," Darnell announces to us all. "Promo reports directly to El Chapo's third in command. That means we are about to get flooded." After everything was separated, we all disperse from the warehouse going to our respective destinations.

Two hours later, I'm at our stash house on the Westside. I got the boah Dewayne guarding my shit with his life. *He better not let nobody break in here and take these fifty birds and 100 pounds. I don't care if it's the robbers or the police. He better let them P-89s bark.*

"D.B., I got a sell for ten bricks. My Spanish boy wants them." Umar tells me while he rolls a blunt of the weed.

"How many you takin for yourself?"

"I'll take five of them."

"Ok, take Brick five, Bay-Bay three, Tims three, my cuz D.B. three, Vanny B. three, and Jambo three." I instruct Umar.

"Alright. And hold ten pounds of the AZ for me. Kev Bell's lil' brother wants it."

"I got you."

I go scoop my youngin Littles up so he can ride with me when I go holla at Big Dawg and my hustling Mami Diddles. Littles hops in looking fly as shit. He's rocking a silverish Prada sweater, some Diesel jeans and a pair of white and silver sneakers. I pay these young guns $2000 a piece a week and take them shopping at the end of the month; my treat.

We pull up on Big Dawg at Auto Zone on the North side.

"What up Romo?" He greets me with the nickname he gave me.

"What up Big Dawg?" I shake his hand.

"This that lime green shit, right?" He inquires.

"Yup. And my man says it's fire, too."

"Can I get the twenty-five pounds for $24,000?"

Is he crazy? "I'm giving you a deal already. They go for $1200 and I am giving them to you for $1000 apiece. So I am giving you a deal already." I tell him.

"Ok, let me give you the stack next time." He says, as he opens my back door and magically drops a rolled up Nordstrom bag in the seat. I didn't even know he had it on him. I popped my trunk so he can grab the box out of the car. He tells me he will hit me tomorrow. I shoot around the corner to Eastlawn so I can holla at my hustling mami Diddles.

"Hey Sexy!" She says as she hugs me letting her hand brush past my dick.

"What up, Dee?"

"You is what's up." She flirts with me.

"When are you going to give me some of that coming home head?" I had to ask her because they say she gives the best head in Delaware.

"Anytime you want it sexy."

Shit, A nigga still ain't hit nothing going on two months. "I'm going to call you on it soon, watch." I tell her.

I handle my biz with her and we go get some chicken and rice from the Getty.

*****

The following week...:

"Thank you so much, D.B." My home girl Marie is damn near in tears after I give her $500 a piece for her son and daughter.

I don't know why it's a big deal. I'm supposed to look out because they are my man Markie Gold's kids and he ain't here no more.

"It's all good, Marie. I just finished riding around blessing

38

all my loved ones with some money. I gave my mom $1500. grandma $1000. My kids, $1000 apiece. Dana, $500. Valerie $500. My cousin Diane's kids $500 and now my bag is empty. I'm just trying to balance out my good deeds from my bad deeds.

"When are you going to speak with my Wali about marrying me Abdus-Salaam?' Khadijah asks me while driving me to the King of Prussia mall.

See Khadijah is my homie Dawood Bey from South Philly's younger cousin. She seen me on a visit one day while she was seeing Dawud and inquired about me. She is a little darker than me with long black hair that reaches her back. She stands 5-foot-6, 140 pounds and reminds me of a Gabrielle Union in the face. I don't know if she got a phat ass how I like because she stays garbed up. She speaks fluent Arabic and knows two-thirds of the Qur'an.

"I ain't ready right now Khadijah. I don't want to be in the dunya (streets) still and bring that into our marriage." I try to explain to her.

Of course she was not trying to hear that nonsense. "Abdus-Salaam, you rather chase them non-instinja making kafir (disbelieving) women than marry a virtuous Muslim woman. I'm not out here humping out both pant legs. I only been with one other man my whole life, my ex-husband. I am a successful realtor with my own money. No kids. Big house and I fear Allah." She lays it on thick for me.

"I do want to marry you and I will, Insha'Allah, but give me about six more months to do what I gotta do. I will make you the happiest woman in the world."

"I am already happy. I want to fulfill my duty to Allah first and foremost and I want to have a lil' Ibn (son) soon. And I love you Abdul Salaam! Can't you see that?" She starts crying.

I grab her hand and tell her, "Please don't do that. You making me feel like shit, Khadijah. I'm going to ask Allah to guide me on this because I'm caught up but I do want to do right. Come on, smile for me." I wipe away the tears from her eyes.

"I'm going to make dua for you Abdus Salaam." Damn, she is gorgeous.

"Oh, I don't mess with no non-instinja making kafirs, either." I smile saying to her.

*****

The next day at the regal...10:40 a.m.:

Torry a.k.a. Big Tee came through the Regal to holla at me. Big Tee just came home after ten years for shooting some Haitian dude. He is from my same hood and we cool. He got a vicious little squad of youngins who do whatever he orders. I want to bring him in on my team so we can really put the city in a choke hold. We're at the same bar sipping OJ and eating chicken tenders.

"Tee, with you and your squad and my squad together, we can do it big. I got all the coke and weed and you know my gun game is up and we ain't goin for nothing." I'm trying to see where he at.

"You mutha-fuckin right cuz. We can turn it up on these pussies. And, I'm trying to get 5th Street back like it used to be. My youngins are with whatever."

"We going to press all suckers and hot niggas. If they want some coke, we gonna keep their money and tell them to fuck off."

I tell him. "Yeah, I'm with all that."

"And, them rat ass niggas get two to the head."

"Yeah, D.B., I'm feelin you Big Homie." I see murder in his eyes when he says this.

"On the money tip, I'm gonna throw you one key first to see what you do."

"Shit, I'm going to cook a half up and bag it all in dimes so my youngins can eat. Then, I'll sell the rest in four halves." He got it all figured out already.

"I'm gonna have Umar drop it off to you later on." He gives me a funny look that I should've questioned.

That would come back to haunt us sooner than later.

Chapter 7

A month later. . .

I'm at home eating Nana's home cooking. I live with Nana now. Just me and her. It's a nice cozy home that I feel safer in than the president feels in the White House. I had top notch security cameras installed all around the outside of the house. Big steel doors with four locks on them, motion detectors, and security lights that light up the whole block if you come near. ADT alarm system as well. Shit has been going well.

I've been out the pen for two and a half months now. We moved the second fifty keys that Primo sent. Now, we just got 200 more yesterday. The whole hood is eating. Brick bought a 760i BMW, Pearl White. Umar grabbed a silver 550s Benz, Black with grey guts. Bay-Bay jumped in a burgundy Escalade. Even Big Tee turned it up with the midnight blue Maserati. The hoes are choosing Westside niggas now.

I finished my grub and am now at the table writing my niggas Chris Ingram from D.C., and Willie B. I put $250 worth of postal money orders and a few flicks in the envelopes when I'm done. A lot of my niggas are in jail because niggas ratted on them. It's time to send these snitch niggas a message and I know who I am going to start with first...that nigga Carl. I pick up the phone and dial Big Tee's number.

"Hey Tee, meet me at the center in ten minutes. I got to holla at you."

*****

41

Ten minutes later. . .

"Holla at me cuz." Big Tee says while we walk down Madison St.

"You remember the lil' dude Carl who told on Troy Kelly?" I ask Tee.

"I vaguely remember the nigga, why?"

"It's a wrap for him. He gots to go." I say fuming.

"Holla at me cuz."

"He work at the phone store on Market Street Mall. I can't believe the audacity of this guy."

"Yeah, he think shit is sweet." Tee comments while eye balling Umar across the street.

"I want your young boy Larue and my youngin Cousin Gee to handle that ASAP."

"I got it. Say no more. Read the newspaper tomorrow." Tee quips.

*****

Market Street Mall...4:45 p.m.:

"Carl, how much for this phone right here?" The fat lady customer asks.

"For you Sue, I'll take $80." Carl bargains with her.

Outside, a stolen Durango Jeep screeches to a halt in front of the store with three masked killers. Two of the masked men jump out amidst legions of onlookers who run to get out of the way. As the gunmen run into the store, they can't help but notice the guy from the Instagram page Tee showed them.

All rat boah had to think before them big guns with the ladders attached to them went off was *Damn, should've stayed down Atlanta.*

The first barrage of bullets tore into the fat lady's face, neck and arm. One bullet hit Carl in his chest, knocking him into the display case. He staggers towards the back, but five more bullets smash into his back, dropping him. One of the gunmen jumps the counter so he could finish the job.

He kicks the rat over so he can look at him then puts the gun in his mouth and says, "You should've kept your mouth shut." As he squeezes the trigger twice.

The two gunmen hop back in the Durango and quickly pull

off. They hang a left down the one way on 6th Street, making the next left on Shipley then a right at 5th Street. Right before they get to Washington Street, they make a right on the short street. They take their masks off and exit the Durango and jump into a green Honda Accord.

As they speed away, Big Tee asks Cousin Gee, "Did you hit that nigga in his mouth like the Big Homie said?"

"No questions!" Cousin Gee answers, giving Larue dap.

❇ ❇ ❇ ❇ ❇

Later on that day...6:21 p.m.:

Brick, Tims, Skully, Bay-Bay, my cuz D.B., and I are laying back at our chill crib on Morrow Street. They are turning in some money they owe. I got $335,000 sitting in the Nike gym bag I just collected.

"They said the boah Carl just got downed at his phone store up town." Tims informs us as he talks on his phone.

"For real?" Skully asks Tims.

Tims signals for him to hold on while he gets more info. I smile inwardly because, this is my squad that I trust, but if you weren't there when the killing took place then you don't need to know. And I live by that rule.

*****

A few days later, at the Regal...2:02 p.m.:

"I just called to let you know that I am home now and I am waiting on you baby." Cooed the sexy female.

"Alright. I'm on my way." I tell her.

The sexy voice on the phone is the lucky girl I chose to finally give all this good dick to after being home over two months. Her name is Latoya Akemi. She is half Black, half Japanese. She is tall like Kimora Lee and phat like Nikki Minaj. She is prettier than Ray J's bitch Princess, so you can imagine what I am working with here. She is an attorney that works at my lawyer Joe Benson's law firm. I met her when I was dropping off a $10,000 retainer fee to Benson. She was exiting while I was walking in and I held the door for her. Our eyes locked for a split second knowingly.

43

I asked Joe Benson who was that Asian chick and he informed me that she worked for the firm. Well, it is safe to say that one week straight of me just "stopping by" to see Benson worked. By week two, I took her out to dinner and it was a wrap. She is open like 7-11 just off the swag and I ain't even fuck her yet. However, that's about to change. She lives in the high-rise condos behind the train station across the water, so we walk there from the regal. Yeah, I said "we". I got young boah Littles with me to hold me down while I handle my business. I trust no bitches until they earn it. I ring the doorbell and she answers the door in a sexy satin robe. I look at her stunning features and those pretty toes.

"Hi Devon. Who is your friend?" She asks with a perplexed look.

"This is my lil' homie. He gonna make sure nobody disturbs us." I smile wickedly as I tongue-kiss her backing her into the living room.

I grab her ass cheeks while we're still doing the tango with our tongues. She lets out a soft moan. She then steps away as she sashays into her bedroom. Ass cheeks looking like two eight-month pregnant bellies. I toss the TV remote to Littles, then I take that walk.

Latoya is sitting on the edge of her bed while I stand between her legs clad in only my Ralph Lauren tank top and Armani boxing briefs. She slowly removes my tank top and just stares at my muscular physique before running her tongue over my six-pack, inhaling my scent. She rubs her nose from my abs to my chest. The mixture of my cocoa butter lotion and Angel cologne is intoxicating her. Next, she nibbles on the tip of my head through the soft material of my briefs. My dick salutes her by poking her on the lips.

"Oh my God you got my pussy so wet," she says.

She pulls my boxer briefs down and kisses my swollen cock. Slowly I'm introduced to the back of her throat. The feeling is unbelievable.

"Yes. Suck this cock. Umm, just like that." I size her up.

A long lick from the base of my dick, all the way to the tip of its head while she looks me directly in my eyes causes me to say to her, "You nasty bitch!"

Up and down in circular motions, she sucks with so much intensity and spit. I'm trying not to shoot my load just yet. I push her back on the bed and strap up with a Magnum condom. I pull her to the edge of the bed while I stand and lick on both of her legs as they're in my arms. I slowly slide into a place I ain't been in years. I'm locked into a slow stroke rhythm. I give her nine short strokes, then boom...one big stroke.

"Ahh shit!" She screams out, but I do it again. (9-1). I keep this up for ten minutes giving her two orgasms so far. I scoop her up by her butt cheeks and lock her legs with my strong arms. Then, I walk her all around the room bouncing her on my dick.

"Oh, oh, oh, I'm about to cuuuummm." She says as she creams on my cock.

All that working out in prison is coming in handy. I put her down and bend her over her dresser and enter her from the back. I'm punishing that big ass, doing the wop in the pussy. When I feel her pussy contracting, I stick my thumb in her asshole. She cums back to back. I fuck her for twenty-five more minutes, all around her room until twelve years could not be contained any longer.

"I'm about to bust." My toes curl and I feel it in my nuts.

Latoya drops to her knees, snatches the rubber off my dick and opens her mouth wide. She is slurping and sucking and I can't take it any longer; I shoot loads and loads of cum down her throat, in her face and hair. Ain't nothing better than pussy except chasing money, so you can get more pussy.

Chapter 8

Two Months Later. . .

Primo is throwing me 200 birds a month. We flip it twice and that adds $900,000 to the $400,000 I had already in my stash. That's 1.3 million in four and a half months. I am ahead of my quota so I jump into the real estate market. I buy five houses and one three-unit apartment building that I rent out. I also bought 100 shares of Apple, 200 shares of Google, and 1000 shares of Netflix. I'm thinking about starting my own commercial cleaning company once I get out the halfway house next month. Umar and I are on our way to Skully's crib to pick up the $134,000 he owes.

"Bro, that nigga Kam from over Southbridge is stepping on our toes. He getting them joints in thru the docks." Umar informs me.

"What he letting them go for?" I inquire.

"Thirty-six like us, but he's stopping us from getting Southbridge's money."

"We went to school together back in the day. That nigga is soft as cotton candy." I say.

"Let's put the press on the nigga." Umar suggest to me.

"We could for real, soft as he is."

"We can go holla at him after we leave Skully's." Umar is ready to get it.

"Ok, we have to go get Allen just in case it gets ugly."

*****

46

We pull up to Skully's crib. He is sitting on his steps crying.

"Yo, what's wrong with you, nigga?" I ask, concerned for my nigga.

I can barely understand his response, "Th-th-th-they killed m-m-mmy baby Star." He says sobbing.

"What? Who?" Umar and I both ask Skully.

"I-I-I don't know. They found her dead in her truck."

"Damn, Salima." I say sadly.

"They said they questioned Ranji, the nigga Kerm, and K.B." Skully drops names on us.

"My man K.B. from around 5th?" I asked.

"Yeah, and they questioned him three times already."

"He's in the halfway house with me. And cuz gave him a job at Regal. He couldn't have done that shit because he was at work all day and night, plus he got to go back right after work because he caught two write-ups." I say telling Skully the facts.

He agrees with me, "I know K.B. didn't do it. That ain't his thing to fuck with girls."

"I just seen her last week at the YMCA. I told her to stop selling pills because young niggas will rob you quick." I relay what I told Star.

"Yeah, young niggas probably robbed and killed her for Percs and Oxys." Skully surmises.

"Damn, she was supposed to hook me up with her girl Kennidy Boyd who moved down D.C." I say aloud.

"She the one cuz. She about to get her doctorate degree and she already makes over a 100K working for the government." Skully tells me like I don't already know.

When I was in FCI Schuylkill with Butter, he tried to plug me in, I wrote her a letter but she never responded back. She is one of Butter's three homegirls I told him I was going to fuck; Claire, Tiesha and Kennidy. I'm already fucking Claire. Now I got to catch the other two.

"D.B. take me over Star's mom's crib so I can see if she needs anything." Skully says.

"Ok. We can give some doe for the funeral."

We gave Star's mom $2500 towards the funeral expenses, but we about to get it back, quadruple. We pull up to that sucker nigga Kam's auto body shop over Southbridge.

"He looks like he's in there by himself. Come on." I say to my men.

Kam is changing the brakes on a late model Toyota and oblivious to the danger that is coming in his direction.

"Killer Kam, what up cuz?" I holla out a friendly greeting.

"Hey D.B., what up, Umar? Scizzully!" Kam greets us. I look around the shop wondering if anyone else is in here with him.

"Are you working all by yourself today?" I ask Kam.

"Yeah, my man just rolled out. Do you need me to look at your car?"

"Na, I came to holla at you about something."

"What's up, D.B.? I heard that you are doing your thing over here."

"Man, I'm chilling, dawg. Niggas lying like shit." *He can't even keep eye contact, so I know he lying.*

"A reliable source said he grabbed two joints from you the other day."

"Man, I-I-I middle man that shit. I can see if my man got some more if you trying to grab."

"Kam, now you are trying to play me. Don't make me take you to get it all." I say as I pull out the duct tape and handcuffs from my jacket pocket. The nigga is so scared he's farting.

"Please, D.B., don't do this to me. I thought we were cool."

"We are, that is why I need only a couple of ones. I don't want to break you homie." I put my arm around his shoulders.

"How much you need?"

"$50,000."

"D.B., I don't got it like that." He lies to me again.

We walk him into his office and I shove him as hard as I could. He crashes into his desk. Allen pulls out the colt .45 automatic and points it at Kam's head.

"Either give the fifty racks or we take you to go get everything and kill you and everybody you love." I spit venomously.

He knows that he is assed out. The $50,000 ain't shit to him. This is a no-brainer.

"Ok, when do you want it?" He asks me.

I hand him the office phone, "Now call whoever and tell them you are about to go to Atlantic City so bring you $50,000 to the shop." I explain to him.

He calls a female I can tell and gives her the A.C. story.

"My peoples will be here in one hour." He puts his head down.

"Kam, I'm going to need $10,000 on the first of every month too. If you getting major money in this city, I'm taxing whoever."

Allen taps Kam on his head with the gun and lets him know, "I'll be coming here to grab that change on the first of every month, Big guy."

Kam just nods his head as the tears fall.

Either you live or die in the most dangerous city in America.

*****

July 4th – Westside Barbeque...3:35 p.m.:

The park on 6th and Madison is jam-packed. Everybody and their moms came out to enjoy the festivities. The grills are burning and the music is being played by DJ Funkmaster Flex. There are kiddie rides for the children. Alcohol is in all the adults' cups and the loud pack is in the air. Niggas got R.I.P. t-shirts on for all their fallen homeboys and homegirls. They unveiled the mural dedicated to Trans Owens who was killed over twenty years ago. A young Westside legend who was only sixteen years old.

The broads are out here choosing for real. Niggas are posted up on their whips, stunting. My entire squad is in the building.

"There's a lot of bad bitches in the building. Amen! A lot of real niggas in the building, amen!" Everybody is bumping to the Meek Millz joint.

My son, Lil' Dev is out here with his boys, X, Dante,

Littles, and cousin Gee. Yeah, all of my son's guys are killers. Lil' Dev is itching to get down but I stay on his ass; got to watch him though.

I got a few weeks until I get out the halfway house for good. They are throwing me a home coming extravaganza at the Chase center on July 29th. Anyway, back to the BBQ . . . A few of my lady friends come thru to holla at me and get a plate of food. Tajuana, Vanessa, Valerie and Marie shake their heads at me every time one of my broads come through. Shit, I ain't got no main chick and I be straight up with all my broads. That is why they love a real nigga. I walk over to the basketball courts to see what everybody is gathered around for.

"Net! Pay me my money!" My man Shep from Danora, PA is on the court talking shit. He got a pile of money by his feet.

"D.B., tell these niggas I'm like Curry." He calls out to me.

"Yea, ok Shep Curry." I jokingly say.

He is 6 feet tall and weighs about 300 pounds. He looks like he can't play no ball, but he will trick a nigga every time. That big nigga can shoot for real. As soon as I am about to shoot the ball, all hell breaks loose.

"Blocka! Blocka! Blocka! Boc! Boc! Boc! Blocka! Boc! Boc!" Two gunmen with t-shirts covering half of their faces came running out the alley next to the day care center.

"Blocka! Blocka! Boc! Boc! Boc!"

They are unloading bullets at the crowd. Everyone is running, mothers covering up their children. These niggas got extended clips that ain't running out of lead. Mike-Mike is on the ground squirming as he holds his neck. I try to make it over to him but I can't because the bullets are flying everywhere. I look up and I see Lil' Juanie and Bundles shooting back at the niggas.

"Boom! Boom! Boom!" I hear cousin Gee's .44 Bulldog barking.

The unknown gunmen retreat back to where they came from. I jump up and check on Mike-Mike. Blood is leaking from his neck. I take off my Fendi shirt and press it against his neck to stop the bleeding.

"Yo, Ernie hold this on his neck. I got to find my son." I

yell to Ernie. I leave to try and find Lil' Devon. I see Brick and Tims standing over Duke who is laying in the gutter with half of his face missing. Next to Duke lays Angie with a bullet in her chest. I see my son on the center steps with Dante and X.

"Lil' Dev, go ahead and get out of here, Now! " I yell at my son.

"Are you ok, Dad?" Lil' Dev asks me when he sees a lot of blood on my Dolce & Gabbana sneakers.

"Yeah, I am good. Here, take my car and roll out." I toss him the keys to my Dodge Charger. I go check on my team to see what's up. Cops are everywhere, trying to calm people down who are hysterical. I stop and talk to Umar and Brick.

"Who the fuck was they trying to hit?" I ask.

"I don't know, but them lil' mutha-fuckas killed my cousin Mike-Mike." Brick says with tears streaming down his face.

"I tried to stop the bleeding, but it was leaking, cuz." I tell my man.

Umar lets us know the grim news, "Duke is dead too and I don't think Angie is going to make it, either."

"Bay-Bay walks up to tell us Trecie's lil' son got hit in the leg and so did Leadbottom.

In total, three people died and eight were injured in the shootout. Somebody definitely sent them niggas to do that shit. *But who?* It seemed like they were shooting at someone on the basketball court. *Was it me?* We have been putting the press down on a few suckas. I got four niggas hitting me every month with ten racks a piece. I hope ain't none of these fools put change on my head. Time to put my ear to the streets to see what's up.

Chapter 9

Two weeks later, July 20th...8:15 p.m.:

I'm finally out of the halfway house for good. All praises due to Allah. Umar, my cousin D.B., and I are at my cousin Darius' crib. His son, Bam Bam, is laying some disturbing news on me.

"Yeah big cuz, the nigga Dahmir from around my way on 2-4 was in the trap house bragging about putting that work in over ya'll way. He said he was trying to hit some old head named D.B. but he missed."

I'm getting beyond pissed listening to this shit, "What else did he say?" I ask my lil' cousin.

"Well, when he mentioned your name, I perked up and tried to fish a little. He said Kojak from 24th and Pine Street put money on your top."

"That bitch ass nigga!" I punched the refrigerator door as I yell out.

Kojak and I were beefin hard in the 90s until I caught him at the gas station on Delaware Avenue. I hit him fifteen times with my tech-9 but he survived; I put him in a wheelchair for life.

My cousin D.B. asks me next, "Do you want me to handle the nigga Kojak, cuz?"

"Nah, I got the nigga myself, but first I want to dog these two youngins first. Who did Dahmir say went with him?" I need answers.

"He took Ty-Money with him, " he replied.

"Do you know where these niggas live at Bam-Bam?"

"I gots my cuz back," Bam-Bam declares as he slides me a piece of paper.

I read the address on the paper, *2406 N. West St.* He tells me that's Dahmir's address. He also says him and Ty-Money go up to Philly to buy bundles of dope together. I tell him I'll give him $5,000 to line Ty up for me. Lil' cuz is with it.

These niggas have awakened the beast in me.

*****

Two nights later - July 22nd...2:22 a.m.:

For two nights consecutive, I studied the whole area near Dahmir's crib. It's a porched house with little bushes surrounding the porch. The block gets real dark at night. Perfect for murder...perfect for me. I know that most dudes stumble to the crib on Saturday nights around 3 a.m. I hear he's on the Percs and syrup hard. *Stupid nigga.* I'm dressed in all black: a black Nike hoodie, a black Sox hat, black jeans, and all black Prada sneakers with black gloves. I don't have a cell on me, all I have on me is one car key. I'm laying on my back on Dahmir's porch. I got my mountain bike perched against the neighbor's house. I hold the fifteen shot .45 tight in my hands as I wait.

*****

One hour later. . .3:34 a.m.:

Dahmir exits the vehicle in front of his house. He made Ty circle the block twice to make sure nobody was layin on him. He's a gun so he thinks he knows all the tricks.

"Hold on Ty. Let me check on both sides of my house to make sure I'm good." Dahmir tells Ty.

After checking his surroundings, Dahmir walks back to the car and gives Ty dap before Ty speeds off in the car. Dahmir pulls out his house keys as he climbs the steps. He fumbles with the keys at the door never noticing the Grim Reaper rising out of the darkness.

"You don't have enough experience, nigga." I tell him, before I squeeze the trigger.

"Blocka! Blocka! Blocka! Blocka!"

"Stupid nigga." I kick him.

"Blocka! Blocka!" Two more face shots.

I jump off the porch and grab my bike and pedal away as fast as I can until I reach McCabe Avenue a few blocks away. I ditch the bike and drive off in the rental.

To live and die in the most dangerous city in America.

*****

Three days later - July 25th...5:30 a.m.:

Bam-Bam and Ty-Money are on their way up Philly to buy some dope so they can return to get the early morning dope money.

"I miss my nigga Dahmir. I had just dropped him off that night. The nigga checked all around the house before I pulled off." Ty says.

"Who the fuck did that shit?" Bam-Bam asks, feigning ignorance.

"I don't know man." They ride in silence the rest of the way; each man in his own thoughts.

My good homie Wesley Player, an old J.B.M. boah, gave me the keys to one of his houses in Northeast Philly. It has a connecting garage. He says I can handle my business but just don't kill the nigga in the house. My cousin D.B. is with me waiting for Bam to bring the lil' nigga to us.

"We can't cook him in here Deen. We will tie him up then take him to the van in the garage." I remind my cousin.

"I know nigga." He responds.

Bam gives Ty the spill, "The papi nigga told me to come to his house up Northeast because it's hot on Indiana Street."

Ty is in the passenger seat counting the $2100 he is going to buy the 100 bundles with. Bam-Bam thinks to himself that he has to get that doe off him because Ty will not be needing that soon.

"Here they come now cuz. Get ready." I tell Deen.

Bam-Bam walks into the furnished house followed by Ty. Bam motions for Ty to have a seat in the living room.

"Papi! Papi!" Bam calls out. "Como está mi amigo." I say,

in Spanish walking into the room with my P-89 in my gloved hands.

Deen walks down the stairs pointing a snub-nose .357 at Ty-Money.

"Shit!" Ty exhales as he stands.

They never take their guns to Philly when they go to cop drugs.

"What's up, lil' Nigga? Welcome to the Terror Dome." I say to Ty.

"That's fucked up Bam." Ty can't believe his so-called boy led him to the wolves."

Bam lets it be known as he retrieves Ty of that $2100 in his pocket, "That's my cousin dawg. Blood is thicker than water."

I tell Bam to go wait in the car outside. We cuff Ty's hands behind his back and duct tape his feet together along with his mouth, then wrap him in a blanket. We carry his squirming ass to the van in the garage. I drive to a deserted block down North Philly off of Girard Avenue, followed by Bam-Bam in his whip. I hop in the back of the van and roll Ty onto his side so he can see me.

"You got down against the wrong nigga, youngin. This is what happens when you try to play gangsta with a real gangsta.

"Boc! Boc! Boc!" All head shots.

Deen and I quickly douse the body and the whole van with gasoline and starter fluid. I strike the match and toss it through the open window of the van, then trot over to Bam-Bam's car.

Kojak hears about Ty's death the next day. *First Dahmir then Ty in the same week, something ain't right*, he thinks. Kojak is far from a fool and senses he could be next. He has some folks down in South Carolina. *It's money there to be made. Fuck Wilmington!* Kojak packs his belongings and rolls himself into the kitchen to tell his wife to pack her shit.

*****

Three days later - July 29th...9:45 a.m.:

All the beauty salons in the city are buzzing about tonight's big party at the Chase Center. Women of all shapes and sizes, ugly to the dimes, are getting their weaves styled and cut. This event is going to be talked about for years to come. DJ Kid Capri is supposed to be on the wheels of steel. Yo Gotti is slated to perform. Lauren London and Pooch Hall from B.E.T's the Game, are hosting the party along with Tyrese, Malaysia and Draya from L.A. Basketball wives. People are coming from D.C., B-More, Philly, NJ, NY, Boston, Detroit, etc., to party like its 1999, like Prince sang.

Reena and her crew of college grad bougie friends are at the hair salon on Market Street getting their hair done. Reena is my cousin Darnell's baby moms.

"Girl, my cousin D.B. going to shut that shit down tonight. You know he thinks he is flyer than Puffy." Reena says to her girls Tiesha, Brooklyn, and Kita.

"D.B. do be having that fly shit on." Kita commented.

Tiesha rolled her eyes and said, "He alright. He ain't all that."

"Bitch, you would fuck him in a heartbeat if you thought he wouldn't run his mouth." Reena told her.

"Girl, bye." Tiesha said, but she knows Reena is speaking the truth. She really doesn't want to deal with any more street dudes.

"Shit, I would fuck him if my baby dad wasn't from over the Westside." Brooklyn adds her two cents.

"Well, I'm checking for that sexy ass Brick." Kita says in a hush tone.

"Bitch, please!" Tiesha burst out on her.

"What are you wearing tonight, Reena?" asks Brooklyn.

"I got this cute crystallized Alexandre Vauthier Haute Couture dress with a pair of calf-high wrap around Red Bottoms." She high-fives Kia.

"I'm wearing a Shades of Yellow Valentino dress with a pair of yellow-studded Jimmy Choos." Tiesha brags.

One thing for certain, these young ladies will be shining amongst the crowd.

*****

Later on that day, King of Prussia Mall...2:31 p.m.:

Skully, Tims, Bay-Bay, and Ibrahim are in Neiman Marcus

trying to find something to wear to the party.

"I like them Trues with the red rhinestones going around the horseshoe." Skully says.

"Are you talking about them grey ones?" Asks Tims.

"Yeah. Do you think them Alexander McQueen sneaks would go with them?"

"Yup, yup." Ibrahim is trying on a pair of dark green patent leather YSL sneakers.

"Yo, I'm about to run to the Gucci store to see if Gay Alex can hook me up." Bay tells his crew.

Yeah, niggas is going to come through stuntin tonight.

*****

Later on that night...9:00 p.m.:

I'm at the penthouse condo I purchased at Park Plaza down by the Brandywine River. My man Umar is there chillin while I get dressed. He isn't going to the party. He doesn't like to waste money on all that Versace shit.

"Why you ain't coming bro?" I ask Umar.

"I'll leave that for you pretty boys. I'm going to be outside the parking lot pimpin. It's going to be a party outside because everybody can't afford the $100 to get inside." Umar explains his plans for the night.

"Well, make sure you keep the hammer ready and cocked when we come out."

"I got this you big punch bowl head joker." He jones on me.

"What? You bird beak nose having joker. You look like Gonzo off the Muppets." I go back at him.

We go at it for a minute before he says he getting ready to drop off some money to our man Maly's sister so she can grab him what he needs when gets to the halfway house next month. I give him $2000 to give her as I walk him to the parking garage.

As he is getting in his car, he glances at the brand new whip a few spaces from him and says, "That's you ain't it?"

"Can a playa play?" I smile while asking him.

57

"You are going to fuck them up with that there bae-ba" I walk back into my condo singing, "I put on for my city."

*****

Chase Center...11:12 p.m.:

The line at the door is all the way around the building. The parking lot is jam-packed. Bitches are out in packs of six. My squad got special privileges to park their exotic whips right in front. They are at the door waiting on me, thirty deep, so we can make our entrance.

I pull up at this muthafucka stuntin! Do you understand me? I am in a cocaine white on white Porshe 911 convertible white drop-top. Everything in this bitch is white except red stitching around the white seats and the customized red momo racing steering wheel. The dashboard is white. The rug is white. The fear box is white. Everything is white. I got the chromed-out Fitipaldi rims sitting in some Perelli tires. I'm bumping, 'Trap Star" by Young Jeezy. Muthafuckas are snapping pictures on their phones. Bitches are screaming my name. I totally understand Money Making Mitch off the movie 'Paid in Full' when he said something about hearing the fans scream his name.

I hop out fly as shit with a form-fitting Versace red tee shirt that has the gold Medusa head on it. Some black Versace pants that has buckles down both pant legs. And I kill them with Gold Strauss Red Bottom sneakers with pony hair on the heels and diamond sprinkles. I paid $3300 for them and I'm the first nigga in the United States with them. Thanks to my girl Rihanna who works at the all men's Christian Louboutin store in New York. I finish the look off with an all-black Hublot that has an iced-out bezel. Avi the Jeweler charged me $30,000 for the piece.

"Rest in peace to the parking lot." Meek Millz ain't never lied.

Westside is definitely in the building. We are in VIP poppin bottles of Rose`, Umar of Spade, Ciroc, Remy, Henny, etc. I'm just poppin Avian bottled waters, but I'm feeling good. A few of my broads are here and they all are lobbying for this dick. My Dominican chick Madeline is looking good as shit in that cat suit. I think the broad Lauren London is trying to holla at a playa because we all was flicking it up at the picture booth. Me and her were kickin it a little bit. And she keeps looking at me from her table. That same look that I've been getting from women since I came home, is plastered on her face. I get up to go see what's up with this chick.

As I'm walking over to her table, I get a text from Khadijah who's at home:

As-Salaamu-Alaikum! R U being good?

I text her a pic of me and the squad ballin. She texts back, OO-thoo Bi-lah hee. She is funny. I smile.

"Excuse me, can I borrow Lauren for a few minutes?" I ask Tyrese and Draya.

I hold out my hand so she can grab it. I instantly feel a sensation I can't describe. We make our way to a cozy corner.

"Am I crazy or did you really wink your eye at me a while ago?" I start off.

"I was wondering when you were going to catch on. I wanted to finish our conversation." She stammers, clearly a bit tipsy.

We talk for about thirty minutes more. We exchange numbers and I told her I was visiting L.A. next month. She says she wants to hang out. We finish talking and made plans then I head back to the VIP.

We partied hard all night until 3 a.m. Then played the night out in the parking lot until 4 a.m. Everybody from the squad got chosen. About three different new chicks cracked to see if I was going with them tonight. I declined but got their numbers for a later date. I told my bad ass Dominican joint to meet me at the 7-11 on Pennsylvania Avenue in twenty minutes. I told my crew to holla back as I jump in my "white girl". I switch to the Meek Millz CD and let him spit how I feel, "I got my city back poppin and they don't want me to leave."

Chapter 10

August 2nd...1:01 p.m.:

Allen and I just finished hittin Big Dawg with 100 pounds of AZ. We are riding up E. 35th Street in my blue Honda Accord when I notice the black Impala behind us.

"Yo, look like the po-po back there. Don't look. If they put the lights on, I'm going to pull over so you can jump out and ghost with these guns." I tell Allen as I give him my glock .40.

"Pick me up at Losha's cousin Shirelle's house down the street." Allen says.

"Whoop, Whoop, Whoop! Pull over, Pull over," the cop yells on his speaker. I ease the car to the side of the street. Allen is gone in the wind like Usain Bolt. The cops don't even bother to give pursuit.

"Fuck!" I let out once I see the most feared cop in Wilmington's history exit the car with dickhead Wells.

"If it ain't Devon Baker." Det. Sullivan says.

"What you pull me over for?" I ask nervously thinking about the $100,000 sitting in my backseat that Big Dawg just gave me.

"Why did your boy run? We only want to talk." Wells says.

"He must've had the guns on him." Sullivan remarks with a smirk. Wells grabs me out the car and frisks me while Sullivan searches my car. He looks in the Neiman's bag and smiles.

"Looks like somebody is going down." He announces, holding the bag open for Wells.

"We seen you make the sell to your man Big Dawg and we

got the money. That's an easy delivery charge." Sullivan states.

"I don't know what you are talking about." I try to say convincingly.

"Don't make me call the State Troopers and tell them to pull Big Dawg over." Sullivan says to me blessing me with spittle to the face.

Wells goes into his game, "We know you ain't trying to go back to the federal pen so why don't you be our Alpo?"

"Fuck you! I'll do 100 years before I snitch!" I yell defiantly.

"Oh yeah, I forgot, you hate rats. That's why you killed Carl." Wells says as he takes off his sunglasses.

This cracka's got a nigga shook. Somebody in my circle gots to be telling.

"Wrong guy." I say.

"Look, we know you are back in business and we know the murder rate has went up quadruple since you've been home. We don't give a fuck, as long as you break bread with us." Sullivan says pointing to his partner.

"You extorting me?" I ask dumbfounded.

"Not really. You break us off and we will let you know if the feds are on your ass or if any rats are in your crew." Sullivan breaks it down for me to digest.

"I'll pay you the money, but I will not be snitching on anybody." I let it be known that I ain't no fuckboy.

"No problem big guy." Sullivan says to me.

"How much is you pressing me for?"

Sullivan confers with Wells, then speaks, "Whatever is in this bag is our first payment." Sullivan says, holding up the bag with my money.

"And we want $25,000 a piece every month." Wells pokes me in the chest.

"How will I get it to you?" I ask the two gangstas with badges.

Sullivan tosses me a burnout phone and explains to me how the exchange will go down.

"I will text you a street location on that phone. At the

designated location will be a black Cherokee. Just place the money in the front passenger's seat. It will be a different location each time."

"Well, for that 100 thou in that bag you got to give me some info I can use." I put them to the test.

Wells walks to the Impala and climbs in while Sullivan drops a hint on me.

"Someone in your circle is working with the Feds. He is wired up and he is coming to do a buy off Brick."

"Who is it?" I ask him. You will know who it is as soon as he opens his mouth." Sullivan warns me before he pulls off.

Brick be serving a lot of jokers all over the city. It could be anyone, but he did say it was someone in our circle. I got to go holla at Brick ASAP and have a meeting with my inner squad. I jump in my car and circle the block to go pick up Allen.

*****

August 11th...7:30 a.m.:

We are sitting in the parking lot at the state prison in Smyrna, Delaware. Brick, Umar and I are picking up our man, Quincy Dorsett. He just finished a five-year sentence. We in a brand new black BMW X-6 that we are surprising him with a little later on. He's coming out of jail cursing a C-O out.

"Suck my dick, Smitty! You boot licking clown." Q was crazy like that he doesn't hold his tongue for nobody.

"As-Salaamu-Alaikum!" I hug my man.

"Wa Alaikum As-Salaam," he greets back.

"What up, my nigga? You picked up some weight." Umar says to Quincy.

"Yeah, I was hitting that steel bar."

"As Salaamu-Alaikum dawg." Brick salaams Q.

Q salaams him back and we jump in the truck and bounce.

I'm behind the wheel, Umar is in the passenger seat and Brick and Q are in the back. It was a purple Polo V-neck, a pair of blue G-Star jeans, a brown leather Gucci belt, and some cream Prada sneakers on the seat for Q to switch into. Fuck those jail clothes. We are on our way to D.C. so we can take Q shopping at Tyson's Corner mall. We toss him three bundles of rubber-banded money equaling $5000 apiece.

We burned the mall up with Q. He buys the new hottest gear. We walk out to valet so we could wait on them to bring the truck. You should have seen Q's face when the valet driver hopped out the X6 and walked over to hand him the keys with a red bow on it and says, "Welcome Home Q."

The look was priceless.

*****

The next day...4:40 p.m.:

Brick and I are chillin in Brick's corner store located on the corner of 5th and Madison Street. He just got a text from Jaylen saying he was stopping by. We've known Jaylen for years and brick has been fronting him a kilo of powder every week.

A few minutes later, Jaylen enters the store, "What up y'all?" He greets us.

"Yizz-o, Jaylen." I holla.

"What's the deal, Jaylen?" Brick asked him.

"Coolin. Just wanted to holla at you Brick." Jaylen says.

He grabs some hot fries and a soda.

Brick ask, "holler at me." I noticed Jaylen is sweating profusely.

"I need a brick of hard, ASAP. I got this nigga down Seaford who gonna spend $42,000 for it, but I don't know how to cook." Jaylen says nice and loud so the wire can hear.

Brick and I exchange glances. We both realize that Jaylen is the rat Sullivan said we would recognize as soon as he opens his mouth.

"Hey Brick, come grab these two $20 worth of quarters out my car and take to Maly over at the halfway house." I say to my man.

"Jaylen, excuse me one minute," Brick tells Jaylen as he comes outside to my rental car.

"Homie, that nigga is trying to get you." I inform Brick.

"Shit!" Brick says pissed off that his own man would do him in.

"Look, I'm going to call your phone you act like it's a family emergency and tell Jaylen you'll get with him later. I'm going to park up the street and wait on him so I can follow him to see where he goes."

"Alright, bet." Brick says.

Everything goes according to plan. Brick spins Jaylen and I watch Jaylen get in his car and pull off. I'm in a discrete Buick Lacrosse rental. Jaylen never notices me following him as he makes his way up near Rockford Park. I park at a safe distance and watch our buddy jump into the backseat of an FBI-issued car.

I call Brick to inform him of what I saw, "Yo, I just seen Sammy the Bull."

Chapter 11

Two weeks later, FCI Fort Dix. . .1:15 p.m.:

"The courts denied my 2255 motion last week, so I am going to finish the rest of my twelve year sentence." My man, Artega "Artie Green" tells me at our visit.

Artie had hopes of getting his sentence reduced after five years in prison.

"Art just look at it as Allah saving you from something because it is crazy out there in them streets."

"I know D.B., but I wanted to get back out there so I could take care of my kids and my get my change back up."

"Cuz, I got your kids. Don't worry about that."

"Plus, I want some pussy badder than a mutha-fucka!" He beams, trying to brighten the mood.

"Man, pussy is the easy thing. It's crazy how them hoes know when a nigga is winning. They must got a money radar or something." I laugh at myself.

"Nigga, I seen the flicks of the Porsche 911. How can a bitch not be drawn to the nigga hoppin out of a drop-top 911 with Versace on?" Art tells it like it is.

"You know I bagged Lauren London, right?" I brag to Art.

"Say Word, nigga?" He says, not believing me.

"Walahi! I'm out Cali in a few weeks to kick it with her."

"Send me the flicks so I can show all my niggas in here. They already think you the second coming of Big Meech."

We both laughed at that one.

"What books do you want me to send to you?" I ask Art.

As he bites into his chicken wing, he tells me to call Joe Joe and get the *When It Hits The Fan* by Wasiim and *Money and Murder 2* by Fred Brown from Street Knowledge Book Center.

Before I leave, I tell him that my youngins will be tossing the duffel bag over the fence tonight at 8:30 p.m. Every month, I get a bag full of cell phones, tobacco, weed, liquor, and Creatine thrown over the fence for Artie and Butter. I hug Art and I gets the fuck out of there. *I hate Prison.*

I stop through Philly on my way home. I slide past the Masjid Muqbil and offer the congregation Ars prayer. Then I go check on my great uncle who lives on 24th and Berks; North Philly. I call Naim and Buttons so they can stop by and drop the $105 thou they have for me. When I finish hollering at them, I go grab me a chicken cheese steak from Pat's in South Philly. While I'm sitting in my car eating, my dick gets hard out of the blue. Damn, it must be all those workout pills I take that got my testosterone up. Since I am in South Philly, I call this freak joint that lives not too far on 19th and Latona Street.

"As-Salaamu-Alaikum! What's up, Karima?"

"What, Salaam?" Karima says with an attitude.

"Damn, you not going to salaam me back?" I ask her.

"Walaikum." She grudgingly responds.

"Karima, don't act like that. I am down your end and I wanted to see you."

"What you want to see me for?" She asks, faking like she don't know."

"We miss you," I say grabbing my hard on."

"You only call me when you want me to do that."

"Where are you?" I cut the games.

"I'm down 64th and Woodlawn" She states her location.

Damn, she way over Southwest. I tell her to meet me at the BP gas station by the airport in twenty minutes.

I pull up at the BP and Karima is already here parked in the back by the air pump. I slide into the passenger seat of her Ford Windstar minivan and give her the Islamic greeting. Karima is garbed up in her hijab and khimar. She is a beautiful caramel-colored sister, but she got too many "numbers" on her. Meaning she fucked a lot of niggas. I know Allah forgives everything except worshipping others besides Him (shirk), but I am not Allah. I waste no time as I whip my dick out.

"He wants a kiss." I say to her waving my dick at her.

She grabs my joint with her right hand and starts stroking it while she looks around the gas station. Once she sees the coast is clear, she removes her head covering and greedily swallows my dick.

"Slurp! Slurp! Gggrrrgghh! Ummm! She slurps and gags.

"Yeah, suck this dick. Spit on it, you dirty whore!" I talk filthy to her.

Karima is an animal! I wish I could just marry her mouth.

"Your dick taste good. Slurp! Slurp!" She says in between slurps.

"Oh shit, I-I-I am about to bust! Ah! Ah! Ah! Yeah, drink that hot baby batter and you better not leave none nowhere, either!" I grab her head and bust all in her mouth. May Allah forgive me.

*****

Quincy has only been home about three weeks and he is moving more work than damn near everybody on the team. He is trying to win hustler of the year. I gave him the second bedroom in my Park Plaza Condo. However, he spends most of his time in his trap house he got on 7th and Monroe Street. Umar and me stop by Q's trap house to holla at him. As we are walking in Rock from New Castle is leaving with a Nordstrom bag. When we walk in, Q is sitting at the table counting about 72K, while his young boahs Ricky and Pac bag up five pounds of AZ in Nickel bags. Guns are laying near. My nigga is going hard.

"What up, Yall?" Q speaks to us.

"Chillin. I see you got it pumping." I say to him.

"Yeah, I'm selling about twenty babies (4.5 ounces) a day out of here. Plus, I got my customers who grab the whole bird, getting about ten a week. And we sell five pounds in nickels a day. That's $10,000 a day in Nicks." He brags.

"My nigga is on a mission, huh Bae-ba?" Umar gives Q dap.   Quincy pulls me into the hallway so we can discuss business.

"I'm going to bring the $670K I owe for the twenty bricks. And, I am giving you $65,000 so I can get 100 pounds of weed." Q tells me his plans.

"Ok, I'll holla at you later then." I dap Q and prepare to leave. As we are leaving, Umar says to Q's young boah Pac,

"Your badass beat that first murder now you think you an outlaw."

"What you talkin bout, Big Homie?" Pac asks innocently.

"Nigga, I know you killed that nigga the other night on 6th and Jefferson."

"Nah Umar, it wasn't me." He lies.

*****

A few days later-September 3rd...8:18 p.m.:

Brick is in his 760 BMW talking to D.B.'s cousin Deen. They are parked on 3rd and Clayton.

"How much your mans Storm and Shannon gonna charge for knockin Jaylen off?" Brick asks Deen.

"They charge $5,000, but I'll tell them I got $3,000. I need it done this weekend. I'm going to the Bahamas with my girl so I will have an alibi." Brick has an air tight alibi.

"The funny nigga be chillin over the Thunder Guards every weekend. We got him." Deen assures Brick.

*****

Five days later - September 8th ...6:21 p.m.:

I'm on the 7th Street side of the park fucking with A-Laws, Mase, MJ, Leadbottom and a few other cats. Skully is up the street talking to some broads in a white Acura.

After they pull off, Skully walks back towards me, "Who was them chicks, Skully?" I ask.

"That was Losha and Kennidy." He responds.

"Kennidy?" My voice raises a few octaves.

"Oh shit, I forgot Dunn, you tryna holla," Skully says.

"Man, call her back ASAP and tell her to come back," I

demand.

Ten minutes later, her and Losha pull up. Skully calls me over to the car. I walk over cool as a fan with some 7 jeans, a white Polo V-Neck t-shirt and a pair of Gucci high-top sneakers on. Waves spinning.

"What up, Kennidy, Hi Losha." I speak to the ladies.

"What's up, Nigga?" That's Losha all hardcore and shit.

"Hey, D.B." Kennidy smiles the prettiest smile I've ever seen. My heart skips a beat.

"What you two up to?" I ask.

"We about to eat some crabs." Kennidy says.

"Why didn't you ever write me back when I wrote you that letter five years ago?" I ask looking her dead in the eyes.

"Boy, I was so caught up with school. My mom loved the letter. She said that you were something else." Kennidy says to me.

"Boy, she is getting ready to be a doctor. She ain't messing with no street dudes." Losh adds her bullshit.

"Shut up, Losha." Skully checks.

"I ain't in the streets. I own ten rental properties." I had to throw that out there in order to quell Losha's hatin ass.

"Shit, they say you said you're back." Kennidy giggles.

"You can't listen to the streets, feel me?"

"Yeah, I hear you playa."

"Do you still live in D.C.?" I ask her.

"I sure do."

"Give me your number so we can hang out. I be down there a lot."

"Ok, its 302-743-8407." She runs the digits to me.

They laugh at my flip phone when I pull it out to program Kennidy's number in.

"You got to get you an iPhone, bae-ba." Losha says laughing, causing Kennidy to laugh.

"I got one, but I don't know how to use it. Twelve years in jail will fuck you up." I admit.

"You'll get the hang of it soon." Kennidy tells me, sincerely.

I think I'm in love already.

"Kennidy, I will call you in a few days, ok?"

"Ok, do that D.B." She says, before pulling off.

"Hey D.B., she is the one for real." Skully says to me as we jump in Quincy's X6 that I was driving today.

"I know, Skully. She is going to be my wife one day, watch." We pull off bumping 2-Pac's 'Ambitionz of a Ridah.'

*****

Two nights later at the Thunder Guards...2:15 a.m.:

The Thunder Guards nightclub is a hole in the wall spot about as big as a two-bedroom apartment. It is located on Governor Printz Boulevard between two of the dirtiest crime-ridden projects in all of Delaware. To the residents of Riverside and 2-6 projects, this is home. You will find all the ratchet hoodrats, thots, and trifling baby-mamas mixing in with the drug dealers, robbers and killers.

The real party is outside the club though. Everybody hangs outside, up and down E. 28th Street and in Booger-Bear's parking lot. This place is the Devil's den. The intersection of 28th and Governor Printz has seen the most shootings and murders than any street intersection in America. Every other weekend some-one's getting shot, but people still continue to flock here faithfully. Tonight is one of those nights.

McBoob is sitting on the hood of Zelda's Honda talking to Zelda, Paula and Rachelle. He peeps Jaylen standing across the street talking to his man, Peabo and some bitches while they wait on their beef sausage to finish cooking. McBoob pulls out his phone to text Deen.

Yo, your girl is here. McBoob texts.

Where at? Deen texts back.

She is standing by the food cart. McBoob responds.

Cool. Replies Deen.

Deen is only two minutes away, around the corner in a stolen Nissan Maxima. Storm and Shannon are masked and gloved up toting two 17-shot Glock 9mms.

"Are you going to let me eat that tonight, Tonya?" Jaylen whispers in the hoodrat's ear.

"I'm on my period, boy." She's fuckin with him.

"So what. That's how I like it." Jaylen sticks his tongue in her ear. The Altima swings the corner on 28th Street and comes to a halt as the two masked gunmen emerge. Tonya looks like she's seen a ghost. Jaylen notices her big eyes and turns around.

"Boc!" Jaylen's head explodes as he crumbles to the ground. Tonya screams as brain matter splatters on her cheeks. Storm and Shannon pump a total of twenty-five bullets into Jaylen's lifeless body then jump back into the Altima as Deen escapes up 28th Street.

To live and die in the most dangerous city in America....

Chapter 12

"Yes, this is Kennidy Boyd speaking."

"You sound so professional." I tell Kennidy, when I hear her answer her work phone.

We have been talking daily, getting to know one another. Kennidy is an exceptional woman. Educated, driven, but also still hood when she needs to be.

"Hi Devon!" she says my name so vibrant.

"What's up? I just wanted to hear your beautiful voice before I went inside the gym to work out." I say to her, as I visualize her dark chocolate face, those expressive eyes and bright smile.

She is 5-foot-9, tall like I love my women. She weighs about 155 pounds, with strong, Serena Williams-looking legs. Her butt is big enough for me to set a champagne glass on. Her ass looks even bigger because of her flat stomach and small waist. This woman is absolutely gorgeous. Reminds me of Kelly Rowland, Carrie Champion, Tasha Smith and Porsha Stewart all rolled into one; but even more prettier.

"Aww, that was so sweet of you. What are you working on in the gym today?" She asks.

"I am doing legs and cardio."

"I got to do legs and arms today myself." She is also a gym rat.

"Kennidy, I will call you tonight before you go to bed, around ten'ish ok?"

"Yes, that sounds good to me."

"Enjoy the rest of your day."

"You too. Bye-bye".

I'm on the Center's steps listening to Cousin Gee tell me about how Littles got locked up last night. It was a shootout at Christiana Skating Rink last night and they claim he was involved. His bail is 5 million dollars. I can't take ten percent to Ted's Bail Bonds without having to show where the 500K came from, so he got to sit in Gander Hill for a minute. I am going to get Joe Benson to represent him.

"I'm going to kill that nigga Gotti from Northside. He started that shit last night. Got my man all cased up." Cousin Gee says, angrily.

"Don't do nothing crazy, man." I try to talk sense into him before he goes on a killing spree.

Maries pulls up in her minivan. "Come on you two, give up some moola towards my BBQ I am throwing this weekend," Marie yells out the window.

We dig in our pockets and pass off $100 apiece.

"Don't let it be no clowns from across town there either." Gee tells her.

"Boy. Bye." She pulls off on us.

*****

Later that night...

Big Tee, Larue, Ronny, Flame and Trigger are standing on 5th Street near the short street conversing.

"That nigga Umar be going in and out that crib up the street a lot." Ronny speaks out loud trying to fish.

He is a known robber and shyster.

"He probably got some work up in that bitch." Big Tee says.

"I seen him go in there yesterday with a book bag." Larue adds.

Trigger knows damn well he should stay out of this plot because Umar is like family and Umar sells him four and half ounces for only $4000.

Instead, Trigger's greed gets him running his mouth, "He served me a baby the other day and he had like seven bricks in there."

"What?" Big Tee and Ronny yell simultaneously.

"We need to go up in there and get that ASAP." Larue screams.

"He got them pitbulls up in there and them dogs are vicious. " Trigger lets them know.

"Fuck them dogs! I'll air them bitches out with my nina." Larue says as he lifts his shirt up to expose his hammer.

"I don't know, man. That's most likely my man D.B.'s coke. I can't do D.B. like that." Big Tee tells his crew.

"Fuck, D.B.!" Ronny throws out there.

Flame lets it be known, "That's my old cellie. Plus he put us on."

"They will not even know we did it. It's a major come up." Ronny responds, laying it on thick.

"Let me think about it, I'll let you know tomorrow what's up." Big Tee informs them.

A decision of this magnitude could start World War III.

*****

A few nights later – Marie's BBQ...10:31 p.m.:

The whole hood is in the building. Niggas are getting their grub on. There's plenty of Sour Diesel and Kush in the air. Liquor is flowing and the music is blasting. The homegirls are lounging all around having a ball. Dice game over here. Spades over there. It's a close knit family-like outing since everyone grew up together all their lives. It's a few outsiders here, but they are cool with everybody. Reena and her squad came through to chill.

"Your girl Tiesha is in the house eating, D.B." Reena says to me.

She is sitting on the edge of the pool sippin on a cup of Ciroc.

"Oh yeah?" I say to Reena.

I walk into the house determined to fuck this broad so I can complete the "trifecta". I spot Tiesha sitting over on the couch by herself eating. I stroll over to her. I see her do a three second assessment; looking me up and down from head to toe. I'm rocking a pair of low top track Gucci's that are the same colors

74

as the Rams NFL Team, A pair blue D&G jeans, and a yellow V-neck tee-shirt that is hugging my muscular arms. I passed her test.

"You trynna look all cute eating that chicken." I smoothly say to Tiesha, as I sit down next to her on the couch.

"Boy, I am not." She smiles at me.

"When are you going to let me take you out?"

"You got too many women for me."

"I'm single as a mutha-fucka."

"I hear you mess with Claire, Neeka, and your lawyer."

"Nah, I'm cool with all of them, but what they got to do with you?" I had to let her know I ain't one of them clowns she dealt with before.

"I'm saying, you out there spreading yourself and I don't want no parts of that." She claims.

"I be chillin. I'm on a mission and I ain't tryna fuck with a thousand broads."

"I hear you, D.B."

I see she is faking like she ain't trying to fuck with a winner. I got her though.

"When you are ready to see what I'm about, holla at me." I get up and leave her speechless.

When all these money making and takin niggas at the BBQ, I decide to round up some money from them so I can send to Willie B., Littles and Gus. I walk over to the spades table where Umar, Ronny, Tims, and Martin are in a heated game.

"Stop talking board, Ronny." Umar warns him.

"Man, what I say? You trippin." Ronny responded.

"You mad because we set ya'll Umar." Tims teases.

"Yo, come on big ballers, dig in them pockets. I am sending Willie B., Littles and Gus some money." I tell all of them.

They all reach in their stashes and drop bills in the bag. I'm holding.

"I only got forty dollars on me." Ronny says.

"Stop being tight R. You got it out in your trunk." I joke.

"Very funny Mr. Funny Guy." Ronny jokes back.

I finish gathering money from everybody else and give it to Marie so she can send it to the homies.

It's getting close to 2 a.m. and people are still having fun. Quincy and I are about to bounce. I pull Umar to the side and ask was he almost done with the ten bricks I gave him.

"I got three bricks left." Umar says to me as he glances over to make sure Ronny ain't cheating.

"Your young boah is keeping watch over them, right?"

"Man, we got into it today and I kicked him out."

"Who watching the shit now?" I ask him.

"Nobody. It's cool, jug head."

"I hope so, man. Me and Q out. Holla back." I give him dap, then roll out with Q.

Meanwhile, Big Tee, Larue and Trigger are waiting on Ronny to call and let them know what Umar is doing.

"I'm about to call this nigga to see what's up." Big Tee states.

"Yeah, do that, cuz." Larue says.

After talking to Ronny for ten seconds, Big Tee gives Larue and Trigger the green light. Larue lifts Trigger up to the side window easily since Trigger is so tiny. When he pops the window up, two pit bulls charge the window growling.

"Down, boys. It's only me." Trigger whispers to the pits while letting them sniff his scent.

Once they smell the familiar scent they retreat and Trigger climbs through the window. He quickly finds the light switch in the kitchen. He climbs up on the kitchen counter and reaches up high above the cabinet where he remembers Umar grabbing the bookbag of coke. *Bingo!* He looks in the bag and is greeted with three perfectly wrapped kilos of cocaine. He searches the rest of the crib like he is looking for a lost cell phone. In the trash, underneath the trash bag he finds two babies (9 ounces) of crack. We will not be breaking this 9 ounces down with the four-man crew. He smiles to himself as he tucks the bags in his boxers.

"Yo, is it cool to come out the front door?" Trigger calls Big Tee on his jack.

"Yeah, come on." Big Tee tells him. Trigger casually walks

out the front door with the bookbag over his shoulder like it's his house.

*****

Three hours later . . . 5:25 a.m.:

"Yo, somebody got me, dawg," Umar says over the phone to me.

"What you talking about?" I say, as I push Latoya Akemi's head off me and sit up in the bed.

"Somebody broke into the crib and stole the three joints." He relays bad news.

"Your dogs didn't attach nothing?"

"Nah, cuz."

"It had to be your young boah because they know him." I state the obvious.

"Nah, he wouldn't violate me like that. I raised the nigga." He tries to defend the lil' nigga.

"Man, fuck that! He did that shit. I'm gonna bang that nigga in his top!" I yell.

"Nah, you ain't doin that."

"Umar, let me rock that nigga."

"He didn't do it! Let me figure this out and call you back."

"Ok. Meet me at the Post House on the Hill at ten o'clock."

"Aight. Peace." He hangs up, sounding dejected.

We are sitting at the Post House eating breakfast with Brick and Quincy while we explore all angles surrounding the burglary.

"I'm with D.B. on killing the young boah." Quincy says.

"He didn't do it! I grilled the nigga for two hours. Plus, he wouldn't know what to do with all that coke." Umar tries to explain.

"Whoever did it will expose their hand sooner than later. We just don't say nothing to nobody about it. It will come out." Brick tells us some street knowledge.

"I can't believe somebody violated me like this," Umar explains doubtfully.

"Once we find out who did it, we gots to kill them ASAP so they know we ain't goin out like that," Quincy whispers so no one hears him.

"Yeah, you right. That's where Markie Gold went wrong, by letting shit slide." I say.

"Anyway, our flight leaves on Friday at 7:00 a.m. to take us out to the Mayweather/Pacquiao fight." Brick changes the subject.

"I can't wait, cuz. I got Avi the jeweler to make me a bangin bracelet with Salaam written in Arabic all iced-out, an iced-out chain with an iced-out door key for my charm." I bragged.

"How much he charged you?" Asks Quincy.

"A bean ten for the chain and charm and 65K for my bracelet. That shit is all VVS diamonds."

"Damn, Playa!" I got to grab me something from Neef up Philly." says Q.

"Yo, I ain't going to the fight." Umar says, as he looks out the window.

"What? Why not?" Brick asks him.

"Cause I don't feel like it. This shit got me pissed." Umar explains.

"Them tickets cost us 44 grand a piece. You buggin," Q says.

"Yo, I'll buy it back off of you. I'll take Lauren with us if you two don't mind," I tell them.

"I hope you fucked her when you went out LA to see her because that's 44 racks on a bitch," Q states.

"Nah, I ain't even hit yet, but while I was out Vegas she bought me a $12,000 Daytona Rolex, so it's all good."

"Ask her to hook me up with the white girl who plays, Kelly on the show with her." That's Brick with his white girl fetish.

"I got you, Tiger Woods."

We all burst out laughing.

Chapter 13

I asked Kennidy out on a dinner date, which will be our first date. I am taking her to Fogo De Chao in Baltimore. It's about the same driving distance with me coming from Delaware and her D.C. We arrive around the same time, 6:21 p.m. and park in the parking garage together. I didn't pull the Porsche out. Instead, I drove my hooptie, a Dodge Charger. She isn't impressed with fancy cars, jewelry, etc. I open the car door for her, yeah, I'm a true gentleman. She steps out in some True Religions that hug her big ass, rocking some high-heeled Jimmy Choo peep-toes. Smelling like Gucci Guilty. *Damn this is the baddest bitch I ever laid eyes on,* I think to myself.

"Devvonnnnn," she cheerfully sings, giving me a hug.

"Wow, Kennidy, you sure know how to throw on." I complimented her style.

"You don't look bad yourself," she gives it back.

I have on a pair of blue Balmain Jeans, a designer rhinestone-studded white V-neck, a pair of white and grey Louis Vuitton sneaks and my Daytona Rolex.

"The food is good here. The chicken is delicious." Kennidy says, as she turns the chip over to the red stop sign, letting the staff know that we don't want any more food.

"I know, this lamb is melting in my mouth," I say in between bites.

"You know, I really thought you were going to be like a typical street dude when I first started talking to you." Kennidy

79

admits.

"Oh yeah?" *I got to hear this shit she about to say.*

"I thought you were going to be dense, but I see how articulate and intelligent you are. And you have such beautiful white teeth, I must add."

"Well, when I was in prison all I did was read, workout and study Islam. I wanted to have my mind, body and soul all tight and congruent." I tried to explain the making of the man before her eyes.

"Then, they say you killed all these people, but I don't see that side of you."

"Kennidy, you can't believe things you hear in the streets."

"You are absolutely right about that. People say negative things about me that isn't true," she admits.

"I can't see nothing negative about you." I truthfully say.

"What I do know is true is that you mess with Lauren London, so what on earth do you want with me?"

"Lauren and I are cool, but I'm single. I would cut her off for you, ASAP."

"Yeah, whatever." She sips her champagne.

"When I was in jail, I wrote down ten things that I wanted in my wife and you got all ten things."

"Which are?" She leans forward a little closer and entwines her fingers and sits her chin on top of her hands to listen intently.

"I wrote down: 1) God fearing, 2) Intelligent, 3) Sense of humor, 4) Ambitious, 5) Pretty, 6) Sexy/Great Sex, 7) Loyal, 8) Honest, 9) Nice Body/Works-out, 10) Good cook," I rattle my list off to her.

"You got it all figured out, huh?" She asks me.

"I can't afford to be out here bullshit'n."

"You're different, Devon."

"Like my man, J.J. off of Good Times used to say, "I knoooow!" We both crack up laughing.

*****

Las Vegas - MGM Grand Hotel...10:11 p.m.:

The Mayweather/Pacquiao fight brought out the A-Lists celebs, athletes, rappers, business moguls, royal families, kingpins and definitely the hoes. Ring-side seats cost a reported $150,000-$250,000 per seat. It's safe to say, that everyone in attendance had money, money and more money. Everyone probably wanted to know who was the handsome young man with Lauren London draped around his arm.

"Come on D.B., let me introduce you to my friend, Meagan Good." Lauren pulls me in the direction of the starlet.

"Hey Girl! I see you in the building," Meagan Good speaks to her.

"Hey now! You look cute!" Lauren eyes Meagan up and down in her Valentino dress.

"Thank you. Girl who is your handsome date here?" She asks while giving me the familiar look I have grown accustomed to.

"I am sorry Meagan, this is my special friend, Devon Baker. Devon, as you already know, this is my BFF, Meagan Good." I shake her hand gently and give her my trademark smile.

"What time does the main event start?" Meagan asks.

"Most likely in about an hour," I answer.

We make small talk then walk around the arena. For some reason, Lauren thinks I'm pressed to meet her celeb friends. I ain't never been a star-struck type nigga. Shit, I'm the man for real. I'm flyer than every nigga in here and I got substance unlike some of these snobby celebs. I go through the motions with her as she introduces me to Ray J, Jamie Foxx, Taraji P. Henson, Ciara and Robin Givens. I had to excuse myself to go find Brick and Q.

They weren't hard to find because they shining amongst the stars. Brick had on a red, gold and black throw-back Versace button-up that Biggie Smalls use to wear, a pair of gold slacks, and a pair of red Versace loafers on his feet. Quincy had an all teal green outfit by Balmain with a pair of cream Gucci loafers.

Both of my niggas were suffering from frost bite from all the ice they was wearing. I was killing it too, with some black leather-type Versace pants, a black Armani Euro-style, form-fitting button up and a pair of cheetah print red bottom shoes with the spikes. All highlighted by the red silk Louis Vuitton scarf draping around my neck. All the chicks were trying to get in flicks with us. I flicked it up with my niggas and Lauren.

"Man this fight is some shit!" Q yells out loud.

"We paid all that money to watch Pacquiao run," I say.

The whole crowd is chanting, trying to get them to do something.

"At least we was part of history," Brick says.

"Lauren, who is having an after party?"

"I think Puffy party going to be the livest. It's $25,000 to get in though." She says.

"Do you got his number?" I ask.

"Yeah why?"

"Tell him you got $50,000 to get us in."

"Ok, I'll text him. He is right over there." She points to him.

A few minutes later she says, "He says for me to meet him out by the restrooms between rounds ten and eleven. He got tickets on him and he told me give him $25,000 too." She smiles.

"Tell him I will straighten him when we get there." I tell her.

"I got this. My treat fellas." She says, before kissing me on the lips. I smack her on her ass as she scoots pass me.

What a life. I love this shit!

*****

Back in Delaware - two days later…

"Yo, did you sell Big Tee any coke lately?" Umar calls me and asks.

"Man, you know I ain't had no coke in a week or so."

Well, he got some, he sold my smut bitch Tracy's brother a baby for $2,000. I know he got my shit." Umar says.

I let him know, "Yeah and I seen Flame pushing a new whip."

"I'm going to ask Kam and the nigga T-Rock did either of them serve that nigga any coke."

"See what they say and let me know. I know this nigga

82

didn't disrespect me like that." I say with murder on my mind.

"We got the advantage because they don't know we are on to them. We can knock them off one by one." Umar says.

Umar meets up with both Kam and T-Rock over the past week. They both say they haven't sold Big Tee any work. Umar is beyond angry and he plans on making Big Tee and his entire squad feel it.

"Yo, meet me at the Regal so I can put a bug in your ear." Umar says to me as soon as I answer my phone.

"Ok, I'll be there in ten minutes."

Umar is already sitting at my table drinking a Heineken. I tell Alex to make me some jerk chicken as I sit down to holla at my partner in crime.

"Them niggas got my shit dawg! They got to get it." Umar says angrily to me.

"Damn that greedy bastard, after all I did for him." I say.

"We need someone from out of town to slide up on them niggas." says Umar.

"I'll holla at my man Kareem up Philly to see if I can borrow one of his shootas." I say as I grab my phone to call him.

"Yea, do that cuz." Umar says to me.

"As-Salaam-Alaikum Reem."

"Wa-laikum As-Salaam, what up D.B.?" Kareem asks me.

"Ain't too much on my end. I need to holla at you about something."

"Everything ok bruh?" Kareem asks.

"I'm about to come your way. Where are you?" I ask.

"Come on up. I am on 12th and Jefferson Street. When you coming?"

"I'll be there in an hour." I tell Reem before I end the call.

About an hour later we are in North Philly talking to Kareem.

"Damn D.B. they took three birds? Somebody gots ta die for that." Kareem says after hearing about the robbery.

"Yeah I need a stray face they don't know. Do you got a shooter for me?" I ask.

"Yeah you can take my young boah down there. He a gun."

"How much he want?"

"Three thou a head." Reem states.

"Where is he at now? We are trying to handle that tonight." I say.

"Do you got a hammer or do he got to bring his?"

"I got one he can use." Umar speaks up.

"Say no more. Let me call him." Reem says, while dialing on his phone.

*****

Later on that night...9:15 p.m.:

The block is packed on this warm night. Big Tee and his crew got it jumping on 5th Street. They bagged up one of the stolen bricks in all dimes and the fiends are going crazy over the size and quality of the dimes. He got Flame and Larue out there handling the sales and his other youngin, Donnie, in the car with his gun just in case a nigga want to act stupid.

"Do you think Umar know we took his shit?" Ronny ask Big Tee.

"Nah, he don't got a clue. Fuck him if he did." Tee says with venom.

Meanwhile, parked in a tinted-out rental on 4th and Jefferson Street sits D.B., Umar, Bay-Bay and the shooter.

"My man next to you is going to be waiting right here for you in the Maxima behind us." I say, as I point behind us to the getaway car.

"I got you, Akhi," he responds.

"We about to ride thru, so I can point them niggas out to you. Take this P-89. It's already off safety and ready to work."

I pass the shiny chrome hammer to him, "I'm going to rock all them niggas."

"Yo, my man here is going to be standing next to them. He will walk off when he see you coming up." I explain to him.

"Ok, how do I get outta there?" He asks me.

"Just run up one block to Jefferson and make a right and run straight down here to the Max." I pointed to show him.

"Got you Akhi."

Bay-Bay gets out and hops in the Maxima. We drive down

5th Street so we can point them out.

"Do you see them two niggas right there? The one with the black leather and grey hoodie and the one next to him with the blue Yankee hat on." Umar says to the shooter as he throws up the peace sign to Ronny and Big Tee.

I drop Umar off on 5th and Monroe and then I drive around the corner to 5th and Adams.

"Just walk up this street two blocks and you will see the niggas. When you hit them run up one block and make a right." I tell the youngin.

"Ok," he says and jumps out the car.

I text Umar to let him know the youngin was coming his way.

"Who is this funny nigga coming up? Watch him." Ronny says as he places his hand on his glock.

"I don't know." Big Tee says eye balling the approaching stranger.

"What up homie?" Ronny asks the stranger.

"Umm where is Jefferson Street?" The stranger asks nervously.

"Nigga it's up there and don't come thru here again." Tee says irritated as he whips the .40 out on the stranger.

The would-be assassin walked away hurriedly. Umar witnesses the entire exchange and can't believe it.

"Yo, this idiot walks up and don't even do shit." Umar screams into the phone.

"What?!" I ask Umar.

"He let the nigga pull out on him and everything."

"Where he go?"

"I don't know where the dickhead went." Umar says to me.

"I'll call you back this is Bay-Bay on the other phone."

"Yo Bay"

"Where your man at? I am still sitting here waiting." Bay-Bay says.

"Man I don't know where that clown at. Wait about ten minutes to see if he shows up." I instruct Bay-Bay.

"Reem your man nutted up on us and he kept my P-89,

too." I say to Kareem.

"He is going around telling everybody up here that I sent him down to Delaware on a suicide mission. I'm going to rock that nigga D.B., Walahi." Reem says, heated.

"We had it all setup perfectly All he had to do is squeeze. He had the drop," I explain to Reem.

"My bad D.B. I'll come do it myself for you." Reem offered.

"Nah, it's cool homie. Just replace my gun."

"I got a three pound 7-snub."

"Ok, that will work." I tell Umar and Bay-Bay what Reem told me.

"D.B., that youngin was nodding off when you was talking to him." Bay-Bay tells me.

"Why you didn't say nothing, Bay?"

"Shit, I thought you peeped it."

"Fuck no, I didn't peep shit."

"That's why he walked up to them all stupid and shit." Umar says.

"We are going to get these niggas, cuz. Don't even trip." I assure Umar.

*****

A week later – Indianapolis Colts at Baltimore Ravens game…

I treated Kennidy to a Ravens game. I needed to get away from the city for a little. Hustling and running around can have a heavy effect on a person. It's a plus that Kennidy loves sports just as much as me.

"I never sat this close to the action." Kennidy says about the premium 50-yard line seats we are chillin in.

"It's only one way to do it and that's big." I smile telling her my motto.

"Come on, Flacco! Do something!" she yells.

"I thought you was a Eagles Fan."

"I am, but Baltimore is near us; plus the Ravens are birds, too." She says smiling.

"Well, I got tickets for the Eagles vs. Cowboys game down in Dallas in a few months. Are you rolling or what?" I asked.

"You better believe it." I give her a kiss on her lips.

Kennidy and I are becoming closer by the day. She is the first woman I can express my inner soul to. We are so compatible in so many ways...I can see her as my wife one day.

Damn, what about Khadijah, though? Allah says we can have up to four wives. That's something to consider.

Chapter 14

After another unsuccessful attempt to send a stray face shooter at Big Tee and his squad, I call an emergency meeting at Nana's house. Sitting in the kitchen with me is Umar, Brick, Quincy, Bay-Bay, Allen and my cousin Deen (D.B.). Cousin Gee is in Gander Hill for probation violation. I decided that we are going to have to do this shit ourselves. We gotta get these niggas out the way.

"I trust all six of you with my life. I know ain't no rats sitting here. All of you have put in work before so that ain't a problem. It's time we turn it up on these niggas. If you get the opportunity, than you got to kill one of them. If me and Brick knock one of them off, we are not going to let you know. And if Umar catches one of them slipping, don't come tell me shit." I say looking at Umar. Then I look into the eyes of everybody sitting there as I continue, "It's about safeguarding yourself. If you wasn't there then there is no reason you should know."

I see too many stand up guys catch a case twenty years later and don't want to go back to jail at age fifty so they tell on a cold case murder from twenty years earlier.

*****

Two nights later on 5th Street...9:05 p.m.:

Bay-Bay is across the street from Ronny making a sale to a fiend while simultaneously watching Ronny from the corner of his eye. Ronny is standing in front of boot-legger Dorsey's house talking to Flame and another youngin. Bay-Bay discreetly texts the hooded gunman who is waiting in a nearby alley. Ronny is standing in front of Dorsey's. Black leather, black scull cap. Texts Bay-Bay.

The gunman tightens his hoodie in order to conceal his identity. He emerges from the alley on the opposite side of the dark street from his target. He starts out in a slow jog that turns into a full sprint as he pulls the .40 cal out his pocket. Ronny who is always on the lookout for any goofy shit sees the gunman coming his way. He never warns his so-called partner of the imminent danger approaching, instead he takes off in flight like Usain Bolt. By the time Flame and the young boah turn around, it's too late; the gunman is two feet away. The gunman recognizes Flame and gives him a pass, but youngin ain't from Westside.

"Boc! Boc!" Two shots crash thru his skull, killing him instantly.

The gunman runs back the same way he game into the darkness. It's war now.

Later on that night Ronny is at Big Tee's house telling him about the earlier attempt on his life.

"I'm telling you that nigga Bay-Bay made the call. I see him texting somebody then three minutes later, a nigga come thru shooting." Ronny tells Tee.

"Them old niggas!" Screams Ronny.

"I'm going to go up on the hill to holla at Deen. I think that was his young boah who came thru here creeping last week. If Deen and them are riding with D.B., we gotta get Deen out the way early." Big Tee says knowing Deen got a bunch of young killers on his team.

I'm on the hilltop the next day waiting on my cousin Deen to meet me. Clayton Street is buzzing with drug activity even though the police keep circling the block. I had to put my gun in Nana's house because it was to "hot" around there. Two minutes later, a car pulls up in the middle of the street.

"Where Deen at?" Big Tee asks kind of aggressively.

"I'm waiting on him myself." I tell him.

He pulls over and parks. When he approaches me I can see

the bulge under his hoodie signaling he is strapped. *Damn I'm naked* I think to myself.

"D.B. niggas saying you and Umar saying we stole some birds from Umar." Big Tee says.

"What? We don't think you did it. We cool, I know you wouldn't do that." I lie trying to throw him off.

"I do not want my name mixed up in something and then a nigga put a check on my head." Big Tee says.

"Nah we got our eyes on a nigga from Riverside." I spin him.

"Somebody came through last night and slumped the young boah. And Deen's youngin came through on some goofy shit, so call him and tell him I need to holla at him. Call Umar too so we can get this shit straight." He demands.

That gun makes a big difference. "Alright." I call Deen and Umar.

I told both of them come strapped too just in case it gets poppin'. Deen pulls up first and jumps out his whip.

"What up? You looking for me?" Deen asks Tee.

"Why your young boah come through on some goofy shit?" Tee asks.

"Man, he told you he was trying to jam someone who left out the Chinese store."

"He act like he was about to open up on us." Tee tells us.

"Man don't come up here asking me. Go ask him." Deen is getting mad.

Both of these niggas are loose cannons so I got to try to quell this situation.

"Nigga stop acting like you are built like that." Tee says.

"Nigga you know about me." Deen smirks at him.

Umar pulls up and ask Tee, "What's up?"

Tee tells him the same thing he explains to me.

"Dude if I thought you did it I would of came straight to you." Umar tells Tee.

"Nigga you ain't the only one who bust his gun." Tee yells. All three of them are arguing back and forth. I'm praying nobody don't pull out and start shooting as I notice a tinted Buick parked down the street.

"Deen that's your people in that Buick?" I ask pointing down the street.

"They with me." Big Tee says cockily.

"Look, it was all a big misunderstanding. It's all good." I attempt to calm everything down.

As Tee gets in his car to leave he says, "Just keep me and my peoples name out that bullshit."

He pulls off and the Buick drives slowly pass us. I see Larue, Donnie and G-Code ice grilling us through the tints.

"Cuz I was about to say fuck it and shoot him in his head in front of everybody." Deen says and I believe him too.

The next night Deen and I are driving down Washington Street, on my way to drop him off at home.

"Cuz, ain't that the nigga Donnie walking right there?" Deen says pointing to a man up ahead.

"Yup, that's him. Get him cuz." I order.

Donnie turns around and locks eyes with me as he calmly remains walking. However, as he reaches the corner of 5th and Washington Street, he takes off running down 5th Street. Only in the movies can niggas outrun bullets. Deen lets the AR-15 go, leaning out the passenger window.

"Tat, tat, tat, tat, tat, tat, tat, tat!" The bullets hit Donnie in his back, butt and legs. I bend the corner and pull up alongside Donnie, as he helplessly tries to crawl away. Deen hops out the car and wastes no time hearing Donnie beg for his life.

"Tat, tat, tat, tat, tat!" Deen finishes him off with five shots to the wig.

"Come on, cuz. We outta here!" I yell to him, snapping him out his trance.

I drop cuz off at his house then drive straight to the train station so I can catch the next train to D.C. I call Kennidy to let her know I'm on my way. The two hour train ride was soothing. I needed to get my thoughts together after the murder. Donnie was one of Big Tee's youngins, so I know he's coming back for revenge. Once I reached Kennidy's house in D.C. I jump on my laptop and check Delaware Online, to see the reports of the shooting. Kennidy got a bunch of calls and text saying that someone got killed on the Westside.

"Who got killed on your side of town, tonight?" she asks me.

"I don't know. I got to check." I lie.

Kennidy looks at me like she doesn't believe me. *Oh well.*

*****

Three days after...4:15 p.m.:

Brick is in the Center playing ball, unaware that Big Tee, Larue, John, and G-Code are outside waiting brazenly on the hood of his car. When he walks out on the center porch, he sees Big Tee and them sitting on his car.

He backs into the center doorway and calls Q, "Yo where are you? Brick asks, urgently.

"On 7th, why?"

"Them niggas sitting on my car four deep on the corner of 6th."

"I'm on my way," states Quincy.

Quincy, his two youngins; Pac and Ricky, approach Big Tee and them coming down Madison Street. Without warning, Q opens fire with a desert eagle .45. All seven men are now engaged in a full scale shootout in broad daylight like they in the middle of Iraq. Cars and stop signs are getting shredded to pieces. Miraculously, nobody was hit by the barrage of bullets.The ground was littered with over 100 shell casings from seven different guns. It's on now.

The next day at the Regal, my cousin Darnell asks me about the beefs that's going on.

"Cuz you got to be careful out there fucking with them niggas." Darnell tells me.

"We about to kill all them niggas."

"Primo says you haven't called him in a month."

"Tell him to just send me only thirty joints this time. I'm going to hit my man in D.C. and split the profit with my team so they can make some money." I say.

Since we at war, my squad can't be on front street making money. Now, we got to find a connect with them guns.

*****

Sunday night-Cowboys vs. Eagles game... starts at 8:30 p.m.:

We are on our way up Philly for the Eagles vs. Cowboys game; Umar, me, Brick and Brick's cousin Fatty. We are getting in Brick's truck but a small problem arises.

"Go ahead Big Homie, you can get the front seat." Fatty says to me.

"Nah, cuz go head. I don't let nobody sit behind me." I tell him.

"Man D.B., stop tripping. That's little cuz." Brick tries to defuse the situation.

"Yo, it's clutch time and I ain't playing no games with nobody." I tell both of them straight up.

We sit there for about five minutes before we finally get the shit straight. Of course, I sat in the back.

Yeah, I'm holding up the dumb ass Eagles sign with Husain's name on it. I knew he'll be in front of the TV talking shit when he sees the sign on the TV screen. I got to represent for my niggas. I am an undercover Cowboys fan tonight because these Eagles fans are the worst ever. I don't want to have to fuck up one of these crazy ass white boys. I flick it up for my niggas in the pen; got to give them something to talk about. And the Cowboys beat the shit out of Philly, too.

The next night Big Tee, Larue, and John are following behind the minivan with four occupants inside as they cruise thru the city. In the minivan, Quincy's youngins; Ricky, O, Pac and Ricky's lil' brother are so busy smoking weed and clowning that they don't notice the Buick tailing them. As they pull over on 4th Street, across from the Chinese store on Madison, they are still oblivious to the Buick parked down the street.

"Pac, get some blunts, too." Ricky tells Pac who goes in the store to get everybody food.

Big Tee taps Larue on the arm and says, "Make sure you kill everybody in that van."

"This is for Donnie, cuz." Larue says.

Larue and John pull their masks over their faces and cock

93

the AK-47's they are holding. They jump out the Buick and run towards the minivan. As soon as they turn the corner on 4th Street, all hell breaks loose when them AK's start to spit. Ricky tries to jump in the driver's seat, but a bullet slams into his neck. Nobody stood a chance of surviving in the minivan. The minivan looked like Swiss cheese by the time Larue and John ran out bullets and fled back to the getaway car. All Pac could do is look out the Chinese store window at the carnage that took his childhood friend's lives.

I got a room at the Hilton out by Christiana Hospital to lay down our next plan of the attack with Brick, Quincy, Umar, Allen, and Pac.

I tell them, "Donnie's funeral is tomorrow and all the jokers are going to be there."

"I'm running up in the church and punishing all them niggas!" Q says in his feelings.

"Nah cuz, its too many people going to be in there. I already parked a work van in front of Donnie's mom house the other day. You and Pac will be waiting in the van by the time everybody come over to eat after the funeral," I explain to them.

"You is a bad muthafucka, D.B." Q says, giving me a dap.

*****

The next day at Donnie's mom house...6:00 p.m.:

Q and Pac watch as Donnie's Aunt gets in her car which is directly behind the work van and pulls off.

"I swear I wish one of them niggas come over to visit. They will park right here too. Pac says to Quincy.

"Cuz, you just got your wish because here's John bitch ass coming up the street in the Impala." Q says.

John navigates the Impala into the small parking space. He takes the gun off his lap and tucks it in his waistline; mistake number one. The back doors of the work van flies open and out jumps a masked gunman holding a Glock-9 with a ladder attached to it. Right before the shots rang out, John realizes mistake number two: Never go to war with experienced killers.

"Buc! Buc! Buc! Buc! Buc! Buc! Buc! Buc! Buc! Buc!

94

Buc! Buc! Buc! Buc!"

Pac stands on top of the hood of the Impala and dumps fourteen bullets into John's body. By the time Donnie's family comes outside, the killers were long gone and John lay slumped over the steering wheel.

To live and die in the most dangerous city in America....

Chapter 15

When I go to the drop-off spot so I can pay the crooked cop Sullivan his $25,000 he is sitting inside the Cherokee when I open the door.

"Oh shit! You scared the fuck outta me." I jumped back scared shitless.

"Oh, not big killa, D.B." he says to me.

"What's up? I need Big Tee's and Ronny's addresses, ASAP." I demand from this pig.

"You guys are dropping too many bodies. They are talking about bringing the FBI and ATF from Baltimore to build a case and put a stop to the killings."

Sullivan gives me the sensitive info.

"That's why I need to get those two, ASAP." I say.

"I'll have the address by next week for you. By the way, I hear that Kenin Bailey is in the halfway up Philly and you know that was Ronny's boy before he went to prison."

"And?" I ask, wanting to know his angle.

"Well, Kenin Bailey thinks Ronny snitched on him." Sullivan says.

"So, I might can get Kenin Bailey to cross his old buddy." I think out loud.

"You are a smart killa, I see." Sullivan smiles.

"Fuck you, copper." I spat as I hop out the Jeep.

I spend most of the week going up to Philly visiting Kenin Bailey at the halfway house. I gave him $500 and take him shopping down South Street I'm trying to feel him out to see where he stands with his old crony, Ronny. By the fourth day, he volunteers on his own to knock his man off for $7500.

"I get out in two weeks. I can do that ASAP. I talk to him every day," he says.

"Oh, we will see what's up when you get out." I got to be careful because he will try to line me up for Ronny.

Niggas are slimy like that. I tell him to call when gets out in two weeks. When I get back to my car I call Khadijah to see if she wants to go and get something to eat.

Just got back in town and I'm riding down Concord Avenue, when I notice the police cruiser behind me. I hit the defrost button then the window cleaner button and finally I press the rear passenger side window button down. This sequence of button pushing causes the sophisticated stash spot in the dash to open. I place the .357 I'm carrying in the stash to secure it. They hit the flashing lights signaling me to pull over.

"Yes, how can I help you officer? I ask politely as they approach both sides of my car."

"Sir please step out of the car with your hands up." He orders me.

"For what? What's the problem?" I ask.

"Don't make me ask you again. Step out the car." He shouts with his hand on his gun. I see another squad car pull over. I carefully step out the car and this prick snatches me by my collar throws me up against the car.

"What's going on," I ask again.

"You are wanted for questioning about a homicide." *Shit, which one*, I think to myself.

I ride in the back seat of the police cruiser in deep thought trying to get mentally prepare for the games.

They got me hand cuffed to the table in a cold ass room for two hours. Finally, Detectives Smith and Lopez come in.

"What's up Baker?" Smith greets me smiling.

I guess he is the good cop today cuz Lopez is mean-mugging me standing in the corner.

"Look, I been here over two hours can I go home now?" I ask.

"I just want to ask you a few questions first," Smith says.

"I don't got no rap." I say sternly.

"You punk ass muthafucka! I should smack the shit out of you!" Lopez screams in my face. He is so close, I can smell the pepperoni pizza he just ate.

"Would you prefer Trippi's or Wrights to dress you?" I send the subtle, but powerful threat.

He instantly grabs my shirt collar and yanks me forward.

"Hey! Hey! Lopez, calm down. Go cool off for a sec." Smith says as he breaks it up.

Lopez grits on me as he leaves the room.

"So, Baker, where were you on October the 16th at approximately 6:00 p.m., when John Brown was murdered in the 800 block of N. Monroe Street?" Smith asks me.

I don't answer him so he continues.

"Is it true that you and your boys have an ongoing beef with Torry Pendleton a.k.a. Big Tee? And John Brown is part of Big Tee's team?"

He is on point with his info. I remain silent.

"My informants told me that John Brown was one of the shooters that ambushed your three friends in that minivan on 4th Street. So, I see why you may have killed poor John." He babbles on.

I put my head down on the table showing disinterest in what he is saying.

"Good idea. Get some sleep buddy because I'm about to go home and get some sleep myself. See ya in the morning," he says, walking out the door.

These pussies really left me in this cold room cuffed to a table.

*****

12 hours later...7:30 a.m.:

"Are you ready to talk, Dickhead?" Lopez comes in the room talking shit. I ignore his dumbass.

"I got an eyewitness claiming they saw you pump John Brown full of bullets that day." He lies.

I still say nothing. This pisses him off more. He grabs me in a chokehold and squeezes me like he is trying to kill me.

98

"You are going to write a written confession to the John Brown murder, do you understand me?" I am losing oxygen and I feel like I'm about to pass out.

"Lopez! Lopez!" Detective Smith rushes in and pries Lopez' arms from around my neck.

"He was about to confess, Smitty," Lopez says.

I'm looking at him with murder in my eyes as I rub my neck.

"I need to call my lawyer." I finally say.

"I see you are one of the smart ones. You lawyered up." Smith says to me as he uncuffs me from the table. I massage my sore wrist while I am locked in a stare down with Lopez.

"Can I go now?" I ask Smith.

"Yeah, let me walk you out." Smith says.

"Hey Lopez, do you remember Dame Emory?" I ask.

"Who the fuck is that?" He asks dumbfounded.

"Don't worry, you'll be familiar with him soon." I tell the dickhead cop.

Dame Emory was a real good dude who was kidnapped over twenty years ago and no one has seen or heard from him since.

Once I call my squad to tell them what happened they all breathed a sigh of relief. They thought them niggas snatched me up. Umar said Kennidy called him worried sick about me.

"Kennidy! Hey baby," I say,

"Oh my God, Devon! I thought something bad happened to you when you wasn't answering your phone or calling me back," she says crying.

"Nah, I was down the police station for fourteen hours." I explain.

"Is everything ok?"

"Yeah, I'm good." I assure her.

Once I showed Kennidy my sexual prowess, she couldn't get enough of the kid. I am feeling her too. She is starting to push Khadijah and Lauren out the way.

A few days later, I'm over my young girl Claire's house selling my man from D.C., the thirty keys Primo sent me.

"D.B., my partner and me can come up here and dog them niggas slim." My man from DC says.

"How much you charging?" I ask.

"Give me 10K a piece and we will crush shit."

"$10,000 a piece! My youngins will do it for $3,000." I tell him.

"Yeah, but they don't know us so we can walk up on them bamas."

"Nah, they ain't letting nobody they don't know walk up on them like that," I say.

"Man, we workhorses so let us work homie." He says.

"I do my own shit anyway." I say.

We complete our deal and hit the highway home. I go upstairs and fuck the shit out of Claire, making her cum four times. We both doze off for a few hours. I then get up, shower and throw on a pair of black Trues, a black True hoodie and a pair of black Gucci sneakers.

I made a $180,000 profit off the sell. I break it down and split it up, $25,000 for my six man squad. Before I go, I sit Claire down to explain I don't want no body to know we fuck around. Not even her best friends.

"Why?" She ask me.

"Because there's some shit going on and I don't want niggas to know I be over here so they can try some bullshit. Plus, I'm protecting you, too." I give her my law.

"Okay, I will not say nothing to nobody." So she says.

"That's what's up."

"Give me a kiss." She is siked like a school girl kissing the star quarterback.

Later that night, I'm riding down Maryland Avenue listening to 2-Pac's 'Pain', when my cousin Vanny B. calls me.

"Yo cuz I just rode thru 5th Street and I saw Larue sitting in his green Caddie." He says.

"Where is he at exactly?" I ask as I speed towards the Westside.

"He's sitting in front of the Farmer's crib."

"Okay, cuz. Good looking out." I say.

"Be careful cuddy." Vanny B. says to me before we hang

up.

I park my car on 4th Street and walk up the short street. I cut through the alleyway behind A-Laws old house. From where I am squatting down in the alley I can see Larue sitting in his car across the street. He got somebody in the car with him. I can't see who it is, but fuck him, he shouldn't be with the enemy. My heart is beating fast and my hands are sweating. I tie the black bandana and pull my hoodie tight.

I start singing, "Many Men! Many, Many, Many Men!" I as I walk down on the Caddie. I raised the .357 cannon and fire, "Boom!" "Boom!" "Boom!" "Boom!"

I hit Larue two times in the back of his head and I hit the passenger two times in the back. I stand there about five seconds looking at Larue laying on the steering wheel before I flee to my car. I toss the hammer in the dumpster at the gas station on 4th Street.

I call my baby, "Kennidy, leave the door unlocked. I'm on my way down." I jump on I-95 South.

I'm on my laptop sitting in Kennidy's bed as she sleeps. I'm checking online about the murder. My phone rings interrupting my search.

"Hello." I answer.

"Someone banged Larue on 5th Street a while ago." Skully says.

"Oh yea. Is he dead?" I ask.

"Nah. He got hit in his head but they say he is talking." Skully reports.

How the fuck could that be I hit him twice with the pound 7.

"Who did it." I ask.

"They don't know. They came out the alleyway on him."

"I guess it wasn't his time." I say disappointed.

I get a few more calls from people talking about the shooting. I am pissed.

I should have hit him two more times, admonishing myself.

Chapter 16

"We got to kill that nigga D.B. because he the one making them other niggas go." Ronny tells Big Tee and Larue.

Larue has been out the hospital a week. He is bandaged up and has severe migraines but he has movements in all his faculties, so he is blessed.

"That nigga switch rentals every other day, so we can't pin point him." Big Tee says.

"He fucking my cousin, Nita. We might can use her to get at him." Larue reasons.

"He ain't going for that. He ain't no dumb nigga." Big Tee admits to his boys. "He came up under D.B. and knows he's a true gangster so he knows all the tricks of warfare."

"We just got to be on sight with the nigga and catch him thirty rounds or better." Ronny says.

"Damn right. Best believe somebody gonna pay for hitting me in my wig." Larue says.

*****

Meanwhile out New Castle…

"Its time our boy Trigger answers for what he started." Brick is telling Quincy and Umar.

"He don't know we know he was in on the shit. Me or Q could just go over his crib and he will let us in." Umar says to Brick.

"We can do that shit now, for real." Q says, all geeked up.

"He is probably over his sister's right now, sleep. He don't come out until its dark." Brick says.

"I'll call him now, let him know I'm coming over." Umar starts to dial his number.

"No don't call him. You don't want your number to be the last one to call him and then he pop up dead, you'll be a suspect." Brick warns Umar.

"Right, Right." Umar agrees.

"Leave all of your phones here and just pop up on him." Brick is the master planner.

*****

Thirty minutes later...11:35 a.m.:

"Try not to touch nothing in here Umar," Q says.

"I got this, cuz." Umar replies to Q.

They are walking to Triggers crib after parking their car a few blocks away.

"Make sure you sit him facing you in the living room, so when I walk back in the living room, I can catch him off guard." Quincy gives Umar the game plan.

"I got you."

Quincy pulls his sleeves over his fingers and rings the doorbell. He rings it for a couple of minutes before Trigger finally yells, "who is it?" from the second floor window. Trigger is a paranoid dude naturally. So, when he sees Umar and Q at the door, he grabs his Hi-Point .45 and cocks it in his waist before he goes to let them in.

"What up, y'all?" Trigger greets them as he allows them to go upstairs in from of him.

"What up Trig?" Umar speaks.

"Yo, Trigs." Q says.

Once they get upstairs, they all go into the living room and start watching Stephen A. Smith and Skip Bayless debate on First Take.

"Skip always taking up for Romo." Umar states.

"I know huh?" Trigger agrees.

"Let me use the bathroom Trigs." Q stands up and goes to the bathroom.

"Do you got the bitch Kia's number?" Asks Umar trying to make small talk.

"Yeah, I got it. What you want to hit?" Trigger asks.

"Hell yeah! I heard she a freak too." Umar says, as he eyes Quincy, approaching from down the hall.

"She let me Fu-"

"Buc! Buc!" He never got a chance to finish his sentence.

Quincy walked straight in and shot him in his head then he stuck the gun in his mouth and pulled the trigger again. Trigger's Hi-Point .45 fell from his waist when he leaned over from the first bullet he took. Quincy bent down to retrieve his new firearm.

"Come on Umar. We out." The two killers walk back to the car like they didn't just kill a childhood friend.

*****

One week Later...2:22 p.m.:

Quincy and me are riding out Claymont on our way to Concord Mall when he gets a call from his Uncle telling him that Big Tee and Larue just kicked the door in at this weed crib on 7th Street. His Uncle goes on to tell him that his cousin Kevy and Skully was right there and they didn't do shit about it. Quincy is going berserk on the phone with Skully now.

"You bitch ass nigga! You just sit there and let them kick my shit in?"

"Th-Th-They had a shotgun and a pistol out." Skully tries to explain.

"You clown ass nigga, why didn't you call us? You let them niggas scare you! You a sucka! Don't say shit to me!" Q throws the phone to me.

"Yo, Skully you should of called me man!" I say in a much calmer voice than Q used.

"I know, I fucked that one up. I'm sorry man." He says in tears.

"I also heard you sold them niggas weed the other day, is you crazy? Them niggas is trying to kill us and you fucking

104

with them." Now, I'm getting mad at this stupid ass nigga.
"They brought a pound though." He says.
"So, what nigga! They the enemy!"
"I am sorry, Dunn," Skully apologizes.
"Next time they come to buy weed you call me, ok?" I ask him.
"Okay Dunn. Tell Q my bad for real."
Skully knows he did some sucka shit. He can't wait to set Big Tee up for his big homies.

*****

Jummu'ah Friday...1:18 p.m.:
Masjid Ar-Razakh is full to capacity. The Imam is giving the Khutbah on Muslims killing another Muslim. He is not speaking from the hip, rather everything is what Allah says and what Allah's Messenger (S.A.W.S) says. The speech is having an impact on all those who are in attendance, especially Bay-Bay. He can hope that Allah forgives him for shedding the blood of another Muslim in this beef with Big Tee and his squad. All over Dunya stuff, too. He is so into the Khutbah, he never notices Abdul Hakim go to the wudu station and text his man Big Tee. Bay-Bay should of went up Chester to Masjid Al-Fajr with D.B. and Quincy, but it's too late. A masked gunman enters the Masjid side door, looks around until he spots Bay-bay.
"Boc! Boc! Boc! Boc! Boc! Boc! Boc! Boc!" He stands over top of Bay-Bay and sends eight slugs into his body. All Bay-Bay could do is cover his head and make dua to Allah. The gunmen runs outside and jumps into a waiting car.
"Did you slump that nigga?" A masked Big Tee asks.
"I gave him the whole clip," young boah Jihad answers.
Bay-Bay's soul wasn't taken that day. Al-Hamdulillah! He took bullets to his stomach, thigh, chest, arms, cheek, neck, and his hand, which stopped the bullet from entering his head. He is glad to be amongst the living. His mom, sister, and cousins are all there in his room when Brick, Umar, Deen, Maly and I walk in.

"As-Salaamu-Alaikum!" We all greet.

He can't talk so he waves. We speak to his family. They give us a few minutes with Bay in private.

"Malik said he saw Abdul Hakim get up and go text somebody a couple of minutes before the shooter came in the Masjid." I tell Bay-Bay what I heard.

"Don't worry, I got McBoob on Hakim's line." Deen tells Bay-Bay.

"He Muslim man. All you guys need to squash this bullshit. I don't want to lose no more friends." Maly says to all of us.

"Fuck that, Mal. It's too late now." I say.

"I'm cool with Big Tee and you all are like my family. This shit bothers me every day." Maly admits.

"Bro, just stay out of this shit. We got to see these clowns for what they did." Brick tells Maly.

"We will be alright, Insha Allah." I say.

*****

A few days later...3:30 p.m.:

"Hey Kennidy, what's up?" I ask.

"Hi Devon! Not too much. What are you doing?"

"I am chillin. I want to see you." I tell her.

"Are you coming down? She asks me.

"Nah. Come up here and give me a kiss and then you can go right back home."

"Are you for real? That will just be too much at rush hour." She says.

"Girl, I'm paying for everything, so why you stressing?"

"Okay, let me see when the next train leaves."

"There is one leaving D.C. at 5:10 p.m. and arrives in Wilmington at 7:01 p.m. Then you can chill with me for an hour and catch the 8:05 p.m. train home." I give her the itinerary.

"Ok, let me finish up here at work so I can make it to Union Station."

"Ok, Kennidy. Bye."

As Kennidy walks down the stairs at Wilmington's Train Station all I could do is admire the beautiful specimen. In her work clothes, Kennidy caused a crime scene because she was killing 'em in a crème Emilio Pucci pants and suit jacket. I am hiding the gift I have for her behind my back as she approaches with her arms extended for a hug.

"Hey sexy!" I greet her with a one arm hug and a passionate tongue kiss.

"Ummm. Hey to you!" She says, trying to catch her breath.

"This is for you." I say giving her a box of skittles and a small Teddy Bear.

It's the small things that count. I remember seeing skittles laying in bed next to her and in her car. You gotta pay attention to the details fellas.

"Awww, Devon, thank you!" She is clearly surprised by the gesture.

"No big thing, baby, come on let's sit down." I pull her towards two seats.

"I miss you, Devon. You are on my mind a lot." She stares into my eyes.

"Well, I only think of you on two occasions...that's day and night." I hit her with some ol' playa shit.

"Ok now, Babyface!" We both laugh.

"Kennidy, we have been kicking it for two months now, but it seems like I've known you forever. Every time I call you I get butterflies in my stomach when the phone rings. And when I'm around you I feel at peace. This tells me that I am falling for you." I say baring my soul to her.

"Devon, I get them same butterflies in my stomach too; when I see that it's you calling. I keep rushing to look out the window every ten minutes when you say that you are coming over. What have you done to me?" She asks.

My phone rings before I can reply. It's my grandma.

"Hi Nana."

"Hi Devon."

"I was calling to see if you was still coming to stay the night with Nana?" She says sweetly.

"Yes Ma'am. I will be there by 8:30," I tell her.

"Okay, I'll just leave the bottom lock off and the screen unlocked."

"Okay. I love you." I tell my Grandmother.

"Love you too Rabbit Foot." She calls me by the nickname she called me when I was a child.

"You love your Nana, huh?" Kennidy says.

"Yup. More than anybody in the world." I say.

Changing the subject, Kennidy asks me, "What's going on with you and your friends?

Bay-Bay just got shot and Q's young boys got killed. I am scared for you." Kennidy tells me.

"I'm good. It's some bullshit going on, but it's all good." I explain.

"I don't want nothing to happen to you, Devon." She says getting teary-eyed.

"Trust me I'm good. Don't worry yourself, ok." I respond to comfort her.

We enjoy each other's company until it's time for her to board her train back to D.C. Before she heads back, we make plans to spend the weekend together.

I stay the night with my grandma since I haven't stayed there at all since the beef started. I slept on the foot of her bed. We talked all night until about 2:00a.m. She really misses my grandfather. All she talks about is going home to be with him and Jesus.

I woke up around 6:00 a.m. to my grandma loudly saying, "Oh, God, No!"

My hand moves towards my .32 automatic under my pillow. "What's wrong Nana?" I ask.

"They just found two bodies in the trunk of that car down on 5th Street." She says pointing to the Fox news live on the TV. I look and see the white Altima sitting behind the center surrounded by police. I vaguely remember seeing that car, but can't recall where.

"Who did they say the people were Nana?"

"It was a man and a woman. That's all they said."

"So many people are getting killed down there."

"You need to stay your tail from down that crazy place." She says to me.

"I don't be down there like that." I lie. I listen to the female newscaster report that police received a tip about two bodies being in the trunk of the Altima. She said the victims were beaten and shot multiple times in their heads. A thought comes to me as I grab my cell phone and call Marie.

"Good Morning, Marie I'm sorry for calling this early. What kind of car does Pac's girl Kia drive?"

"Uh, she drives a white Altima, Why?" She asks.

"Turn on the news. They found two bodies in the trunk of a white Altima. Let me call Q and I'll hit you back." I tell her.

I call Q's phone six times, but it goes to voicemail. I get up and drive down there to see what's up.

A few minutes later I walk up on a small crowd of people who are standing across the street consoling Pac's sister, Wanda, who is crying hysterically.

"What up y'all?" I greet the familiar neighborhood faces.

"They killed Pac, D.B.!" Stella says to me.

"Fuck!" I say. I call Q again and he answers half asleep.

"Man, they found Pac and a girl dead in a trunk of a car." I deliver the bad news to Quincy.

"What! Where at?" Q asks, now fully awake.

"I'm on 5th down bottom."

"I'm on my way." Q informs me.

An hour later, we are all standing on the corner of 5th and Monroe. Quincy, Brick, Umar Deen, Allen and Me. We are watching the cops work at the crime.

"Yo, my mom is stressing over all this beefing. She's scared somebody might run up in our crib looking for me and hurt my family." Allen says to us.

"Shit, I'm tired of looking over my shoulder 24/7," Brick says.

"Man, I take a shower with my gun sitting on the edge of the tub and take a shit with my gun, too." I say to my squad.

This beef is taking a toll on us and our families. However; it just intensified by them killing Pac. All four of Quincy's young boah's are dead and he is ready to kill any and everybody.

"I got to make sure my youngin gets sent off in style. That was a real nigga." Q says.

"Yeah, let his peoples know we will pay for everything." I tell Q.

"From now on everywhere any of you go, make sure you call somebody in the crew to let them know where you're going and who you are with." Brick tells us.

Chapter 17

One month later...10:40 a.m.:

Both sides of the beef are being extra careful. Nobody wants to be the next homicide victim. There have been nine fatalities attributed to the bloody neighborhood feud. Everybody is playin the outskirts of the city, not venturing to the Westside. Just to get a drink, niggas are going to Irish bars out Newark or going to the movies way out Granite Run Mall. So, when Nana called me to come shovel the snow off her sidewalk and steps, I should've got my sons to do it because of the possible dangers.

"That nigga ain't gonna be at his grandmom's crib. I ride pass there every day looking for him." Ronny says to Big Tee, as they ride towards my grandmom's house with the young boah, Jihad.

"Man, he loves his grandma, so he going to make sure the snow gets shoveled." Tee explains.

"Fuck it. Let's see." Ronny says.

I am paranoid like shit. I keep looking all around and up and down the street. I have my .32 automatic out, tucked under my armpit while I am shoveling.

"Look! I told you! I told you he would be out there shoveling that snow!" Big Tee jumps up and down in his seat, animated.

"I'm going to pull around the corner." Ronny says.

"Yo, Jihad, that alleyway leads straight in front of his crib. Shoot that nigga ten times in his face." Tee hypes his youngin

111

up.

"I got you, cuz." Jihad says and hops out the whip. Jihad gets a clear view of me across the street with my back turned.

He also sees the black gun under my arm, too, so he knows he gotta catch me off guard. He creeps nearer to where I am and crouches behind a car. I look around because I thought I heard a noise behind me. Seeing nothing, I go back to shoveling, Jihad makes his moves and jumps out on me and aims the Sig Saurer .45 at my head and pulls the trigger.

"Click!" The clicking noise alarms me to danger and I swing my elbow into the gut of the gunman. I grab his hand that's holding the gun and we start wrestling. My .32 drops from under my arm, to the ground. The lil' nigga is strong as a bull with fresh, out of prison strength. I hit that nigga with a right uppercut that drops him on his ass as his gun flies out of his hand and into the snow. I hurriedly pick up my gun and put it to his head as I look to make sure ain't no nosey neighbors looking.

"Devon! No! Jesus, please don't shoot that boy!" My grandma screams from the porch.

I turn to see the petrified look on her face. I look Jihad in his eyes and I don't see no fear in his eyes, even with a gun in his face. *This nigga just tried to kill me*, I think to myself. I hit the nigga with all my might, across the bridge of his nose with the butt of the gun. Blood spurts out, all over my Polo boots and snow. The nigga gets up and hauls ass through the alley. I grab his gun off the ground and run to my car. I tell my grandma to lock up and cut the ADT on. I race out of there to go find my squad. That nigga Jihad will not live to see his next birthday. I promise that.

*****

Three days later...5:25 p.m.:

Brick and I are parked on 8th and Lombard Street while we listen to Tims speak to G-Code on speakerphone.

"Yom the big homie said he got five racks for you if you still gonna handle that." Tims tells G-code.

"Yeah, bruh. I'm trying to handle that." G-Code claims.

"I'm not really convinced that this nigga G-Code would cross his man's Larue and Big Tee like that. I whisper to Brick, "I don't believe that shit."

"Let him see what he can do for us." Brick says to me.

"You sure you can do that to your boys?" Tims asks him.

"Man, Tee ain't playin fair. He ain't feedin me like he should. I want the block for myself, anyway." G-Code says.

"When can you do it?" Brick says. "Shit, I can do it later on tonight, if you want." G-Code says.

I shake my head no to Brick, hoping to alleviate this play. I smell the double-cross.

"Listen, we will hit you back later on to see what's up." Brick spins him.

"Ok, do that Big Homie," G-Code says before he hangs up.

"Yo, he with them, cuz. He ain't killin his man Tee." I say to the both of them.

"Nah, he is dead serious Big Homie." Tims says.

He sure has faith in this dude. Tims don't know that I know he is still hanging around Ronny. I got to watch him too.

"We should call him back and tell him to meet us and kill him for trying to be slick." Brick throws out there.

I make eye contact with Brick through the rearview mirror, nodding my head at Tims. We can't involve him in our plots because he is playing fifty. We pull off, headed to drop Tims off.

That night, I get a call from Kennidy all in her feelings.

"Why I get a call from my folks telling me that the bitch Claire is up in the hair salon saying she messes with you? And how you be over her house almost every night." She says.

"Aww, are you jealous?" I tease her.

"Yo, stop playin with me, D.B. You not gonna be fuckin all these hoes on my watch!" She barks.

"Do you want me to leave her alone? Just say it." I challenge her.

"Yeah, I want you to leave her alone." Kennidy says, after some thought.

"Ok, I am about to go handle that now." I tell her, before

we hang up.

I'm not just going to cut Claire off because of Kennidy only, but mostly because she could of put me in danger by running her mouth. Her crib was a safe haven for me.

I listen to Claire claim she didn't say anything to anybody. The jury might believe her and the crocodile tears, but a seasoned vet like me ain't trying to hear it.

"I didn't let anyone know we was messing around. Not even my boys." I tell her.

"Just give me one more chance. I promise, I will not say nothing." Claire says.

"Nah, I can't fuck with you like that no more. It's clutch time and I can't trust nobody." I return her house key she gave me and walk out the door leaving Claire in her thoughts. I call Kennidy as soon as I pull off in my car.

"Done deal." I say, soon as she answers her phone.

"Stop lying, boy. You didn't cut her off just like that." Kennidy says.

"Call me back once you realize I'm a real nigga." I bang the phone on her.

Ten seconds later, Kennidy is calling me back.

I'm the man, I think to myself.

Chapter 18

Arlington, TX-AT&T Stadium: Eagles vs. Cowboys...
8:50 p.m.:

We are sitting up in $1100, 50-yard line seats, at the game of the year. Winner takes the Division and gains home field advantage for next week's divisional playoff game between the two. Kennidy has on a pink and white Eagles hat, with a McNabb jersey on. Umar has on Brian Dawkins Eagles jersey. I have a blue and white Cowboys hat on and matching jacket. I can't help but to marvel at how nice the stadium is. The big screen is the largest television in the world. I gots to brag to these two bum ass Eagles Fans.

"How does it feel to be in the best stadium in the NFL?" I brag to my guests.

"Only thing nice is the TV screen." Kennidy is a hater.

"This shit is trash man." Umar says.

"Look how comfy it is compared to the Eagles stadium." I say to Umar.

My phone vibrates and I see it's my man Stacy calling from prison.

"Hip Dude! I know you at the game, ain't you?" Stacy asks in his Midwest accent.

"You know it, Hip Dude! I'm flickin it up, just like you want."

"Make sure you get some shots of the cheerleaders, too. Touchdown!!!" He screams in my ear after Dallas scores.

"Stacy, call me tomorrow, because it is loud as shit in here. I'm about to talk shit to my girl."

"Ok, Hip Dude! Peace!"

Dallas manhandles Philly. 24-0 and Kennidy and Umar got their shit faces on.

"Take that Eagles shit off while you walking with me." I say to them.

"Screw you Pal." Kennidy says in her white boy voice.

"Can I get my $100 brother?" I stick my hand out to Umar.

"Here meat head, take your measly $100." Umar says.

Kennidy snuggles close to me as we hold hands walking to the car.

"Your girl Claire came in the salon sad because you left her alone. She said you told her you can't fuck with her no more, because she runs her mouth." Kennidy says with contentment.

"Damn, you got spies everywhere. You get info quick," I say.

"Yeah, so you better not try to play me, either." She tells me.

I reply, by kissing her like she is my wife.

*****

Later that week...4:06 p.m.:

My cousin Darius and I are smoking some Kush over our people's Alex's crib on 6th and Washington Street. Yeah, I started smoking weed again once this beef heated up. I was stressed out, feeling like I was on borrowed time.

"Cuddy, I got some people in the yard you can send for and they will murder them clowns for you." Darius says.

"Man, them yard niggas can't fuck with me and my crew." I say, just to fuck with him because he thinks Jamaicans are the best at everything.

"Yeah, so why the boah Ronny still breathing then?" He asks.

"The same reason his man, Donnie ain't breathing; the Qadr of Allah." I say.

Meanwhile, Umar is at the red light on 9th and Adams Street when he notices Big Tee and Larue pull up two cars back in the other lane.

"Yo, there go that nigga Umar up at the light." Larue says. He immediately jumps out the car, gun in hand. Ave peeps him as the light turns green. He hits the gas pedal and speeds away onto I-95. Big Tee speeds off in pursuit. Tee is gaining on Umar as Umar jumps off the Concord Avenue exit with Tee right behind. Umar barrels down Concord Avenue and bangs a left onto Washington Street.

"Yo, them niggas is chasin me in my car!" Umar yells into the phone.

"Where are you?" I frantically ask him. "I'm on Washington Street," he says.

I'm on 6th and Washington, so I haul ass outside and hide in an alley on Washington Street.

"Yo, ride down towards 6th Street. I am in the alley. I am going to light their asses up." I tell him.

"I'm all the way up 26th and Washington." He lets me know his location.

"Yo, I'm on my way." I race off in my car. I call Deen and Q to let them know what's up and to go over Northside, ASAP.

Umar calls back, "I lost them niggas. Them bitch ass niggas was point'n their guns out the window, but they couldn't get a clean shot at me." He explains.

"Meet me over Dana's crib." I tell him. Umar is driving with Quincy in the passenger seat. Deen and I are in the rear. We armed to the teeth. Umar has a 9mm on his lap. Qunicy is holding a .40 cal. I got a 15-shot on me and Deen got the Mac-11. We are riding around looking for these niggas. Deen gets a call from his barber at A.G.T. barbershop, that Ronny is in the barber's chair and Tee is telling him how he just chased Umar.

"Yo, them niggas are all up A.G.T." Deen says.

We are parked a block up from the barbershop on Lancaster Ave, scooping the scene.

"D.B. and Q will run in there shooting while I'll come through the back door." Deen says.

"Nigga, they will see us coming a mile away." I say to my

cousin.

"Nah, me and D.B. can post up in the alley down the street so when they come down Lancaster, we catch them at the light." Q comes up with a good idea.

"Ok, let's go, Q. Umar, call us when they are coming our way." I tell Umar.

We are waiting in the alleyway with our hoods tight around our faces with ski masks on. While we are laying wait on our prey, a lady comes out to her back yard to take out the trash.

"Hey, what are you two doing? Get away from here!" She yells at us.

"Shit! We got to bounce; come on." Q says to me.

While we are distracted by this lady, I miss the call from Umar telling us that they are at the red light. Once Q and I are back in the car, we get into an argument with Deen about the missed opportunity. We drop Deen off to his crib. We ride around the city looking for these niggas with no luck. They seem to have just vanished.

"Yo, I'm hungry as a muthafucka." Q announces.

"Do you want chicken and rice from the Getty?" Umar asks us.

"Nah, that place is too hot. Let me call Vanny B. to see if he cooked anything." I suggest.

I call my cousin but he says he isn't home. Umar decides to go to McDonald's on 40th and Market. The drive through is long as shit, but a hungry nigga gotta do what he got to do. I decide to call Kennidy to hear her voice.

"Hey sexy," I say to her.

"Hi Devon! What are you up to?" She asks me.

"I'm chillin, with Umar and Q. We about to get some McDonald's."

"Yuck. I hope you aren't getting any beef." She says.

"Hey, ain't that the bitch Patrese car Q fucks with?" Big Tee says to Larue as they coast pass the McDonald's. They both squint their eyes trying to peer into the heavily tinted vehicle.

"That's Umar driving. Park behind McDonald's." Larue tells Tee.

"Kennidy, let me call you back." I say.

"Why?"

"Something don't feel right. I'll call you back. I love you." I tell Kennidy.

My sixth sense can feel something ain't right.

"Awww. I love you." Q teases me.

"What you want to eat jug head?" Umar asks me.

"Get me two fish sandwiches with cheese, some fries and a Vanilla shake." We place our orders and slide up in the line. We are listening to Gucci Mane on the radio. Each of us are in our own world when the back windshield shatters.

"Boc! Boc! Tat! Tat! Tat! Boc! Tat! Tat! Boc!"

"Oh shit! Where they at?" I yell as I lean over in Umar's lap and start firing my .45 out the passenger window.

I see Q laying down across the backseat, firing over his shoulder through the back window.

"Boc! Boc!"

"Pop! Pop! Pop!"

"Tat! Tat!"

"Boc! Boc! Boc!"

"Pop! Pop! Pop! Boc! Boc!"

We are trying to keep them off our asses. I look up and see that Umar got shot in his head and he is leaned up against the window, *dead*. I feel a burning sensation in my arm and shoulder. I try opening my door but I can't get it opened. The car is getting riddled with bullets. All of a sudden, Umar wakes up and crashes us through two cars.

"Ouch, I got hit in the back, Bro." Umar says. I am checking my head to see if I got hit because my ears are ringing.

"Q, are you hit?" I ask Q.

"Nah, I am good." He answers.

Umar's head is leaking blood everywhere as he cuts through the Shell gas station. He crashes into a gas pump, but manages to control the car. When we turn onto Lea Boulevard, we crash into Big Tee's car as they were racing away. Quincy falls out of the car on impact.

"Boc! Boc!" I hear a few more shots.

"Go! Go! Go!" I tell Umar, but he keeps nodding out. I had to grab the wheel a few times.

"Bro, this shit hurts." Umar says in pain.

"Yo, go up here and make a left. Claire can take us to the hospital." I tell Umar.

Umar parks the bullet-riddled car and I grab both of our guns and help Umar out of the car. I bang on Claire's door until she answers and lets us in.

"Devon, is he ok? She asks.

"Come on, take us to the hospital." I tell her. She helped me get Umar into her truck.

Quincy calls me, "Yo, come get me, man. I dropped my hammer and its cops all over." He says urgently.

"We are hit and Umar got hit in his head. We got to get him to the hospital."

"D.B., please come get me." Q begs.

"Where are you?"

"I'm in the woods by White Glove." I tell him we are on the way.

Claire drives us to pick up Q. She tells me to keep talking to Umar to keep him alert.

"Bro, stay up, man. Don't die on me." I say to Umar.

Q jumps in the car and I hand him Umar's gun.

"How did you fall out the car, Q?" Umar says very weakly.

"Man the door just flew open." Q tells us.

I call Umar's girl and hand him the phone so he can talk to her. Then I call Kennidy to let her know I got shot and we are on our way to Christiana Hospital. We drop Q off on 7th and Washington before we get to the hospital. I stash the hammer in the bushes at Olive Garden and tell Claire to come back and get it for me. She is a trooper because she never panicked and did exactly what she was told to do. When I carried Umar through the double doors of the hospital, he lost con-sciousness and collapsed.

"Hey, somebody help us! Help!" I yelled at the slow ass nurses behind the desk. I wasn't even concerned about my two bullet wounds; I was just hoping that my best friend makes it.

Chapter 19

After getting out the hospital, I decided it was a good idea to lay low so I could recuperate and get my mind right. Getting shot will make a man reevaluate his life. I can dish out the bullets, but taking them is something I don't want to experience again. Then being trapped inside a car that is being riddled with bullets is very frightening. I was asleep the other night in bed with Kennidy and woke up screaming. Sweat was pouring down my face and my shirt was drenched. I can't get caught slipping again for sure.

Umar survived the ambush, but he had to stay in the hospital a week because the doctors had to run a series of tests due to the head wound. He is laying low at his crib out in the suburbs. We are all at his house smoking and drinking. Umar and Vanny B. are playing Madden on Play station, while Quincy and Deen are rolling more blunts. I'm using Umar's money counting machine to count the forty racks I just got from my ma, Buttons.

"What are you doing for your birthday D.B.?" Vanny B. asks me.

"You know Muslims don't celebrate birthdays, but I am taking Kennidy to South Beach. We are staying at the Ritz Carl in the Penthouse suite." I tell my cousin.

"I like Kennidy cuz. That's my peoples." Deen says.

"Yeah, that's my baby." I admit.

"Next! That's 21-0, nigga! Next!" Umar rejoices his

121

victory in Madden.

I call my baby mom Cheryl to tell her to meet me at the Wawa so I can give her this $90,000 to put up until I get back from Miami.

"Cheryl, what up?"

"Ain't shit. Chillin." She says.

"I need to holla at you. Meet me at the Wawa on Rt. 13 so I can give you something." I tell her.

"When?"

"Can you meet me in twenty minutes? I ask her.

"Yeah."

"Okay, Bye." I hang up the phone, grab my pistol and the money and head out the door.

I'm pumping gas as Cheryl pulls up with a car full of her friends smoking weed. I definitely can't pass off the money in front of her girls and I'm not giving her my money to ride with and the car smells like Snoop Dogg meets Bob Marley.

"What's up, Devon?" Cheryl asks as she gets out her car.

"I wanted you to hold this money for me, but you brought them hoes with you." I tell her.

"Just put it in the trunk." She says.

"Nah, it's cool, I'll put it up. Do you need a few dollars?" I ask her.

"I ain't never going to turn down no money." She sticks her hand out. I give her $200 before I head back to Umar's house.

When I arrive back at Umar's house, I call Kennidy to let her know I'll be there to pick her up from her mom's house in an hour. Our plane leaves at 7:00 a.m. tomorrow, so we are staying at a hotel next to the airport in Philly. I got to figure out where to put this money before I leave.

"Yo, Umar, can I keep my money here until I get back?" I ask.

"Yeah, jug head. My crib is safer than Fort Knox." He says.

He has an elaborate security system equipped with cameras surrounding his house. I decide to leave the money under the couch in the den. Before we all leave Q gives Umar a .357 so he can calm his nerves. Umar said he felt naked without any protection.

*****

Early the next morning. . .

Kennidy and I are on our way to catch our flight when I get a call from mom dukes.

She hits me with some disturbing news, "Dev, the policed just raided mom's house. She said it's like thirty cops tearing the house up. Don't get on that plane."

"Why they say they came?" I ask.

"I don't know. I'm on my way over there now." She says.

"Do you think they waiting at the airport?" I ask my mom.

"Boy, go somewhere and chill until I call you back."

"Okay, call me back." I hang up and tell Kennidy the bad news.

Five minutes later, my mom calls me back to tell me that the cops ran up in Umar's crib, too. She said they found a gun and $157,000 cash in his crib. I'm in our hotel room smoking blunt after blunt trying to wrap my head around what's going on. I call Umar's girl and she said the cops were looking for guns and drugs. My grandma's house was clean as an ashtray in the Pope's limo, so I wasn't worried about another charge.

A week later, I go see my probation officer for my monthly visit. I had to let my P.O. know about me being shot and about the cops raiding my house.

"Hi Mr. Baker, come in. Have a seat." My P.O. points to the chair in front of his desk. I sit down and begin to tell him about me getting shot.

"I was on my way to my anger management class with my friend. We were in McDonald's drive-thru, when somebody shots us." I say careful to leave certain parts out.

"Who shot you?" My P.O. asks.

"I don't know." I lie.

"Where were you shot at?"

"I was hit in my arm and shoulder." I reply.

He is acting like he didn't know I got shot when it was all on the news and in the newspapers. His office phone rings after he grills me with a thousand questions. He speaks to the caller, briefly then hangs up and resumes the questions. A few minutes later, there's a knock at the door. I look up to see an FBI agent and a homicide detective enter the office.

"Mr. Baker, can you stand up and put your hands behind your back? You are under arrest." The homicide detective says to me.

"For what?" I look at the asshole.

"For possession of a firearm by a convicted felon, possession of ammunition, discharging a firearm on a city street, and possession of a firearm during the commission of a felony." He runs down a slew of charges.

"What? When did I get caught with a gun?" I ask while being placed in handcuffs.

"When you were firing your handgun at your assailants during the shoot-out at the McDonald's," the cop replies.

"No, I didn't! I'm the victim!" I try to explain.

"Mr. Baker, call me as soon as you are released." My dickhead P.O. tells me.

"Yeah, whatever." I say to him as I'm led out the office in cuffs.

I was released on bail after being question by the detectives about all the murders on the Westside. Once they seen that I was not going to cooperate, they left me alone. The charges against me and Umar were bullshit. The cops based their case off of the spent shell casings they found in our car. The shooters had to be close enough that their shells dropped in our car. Joe Benson will eat this case up.

Umar was only out on bail for one week before the Feds pick up the gun case against him. With my partner off the streets, we were left shorthanded in the war against Big Tee and his squad.

I'm riding with Q in his Challenger rental on our way to holla at Brick.

"I got Benson to represent Umar." I told Q.

"He'll probably get three years for that shit." I say.

"Damn, he just got that hammer that night. What they say about all that money?" Q asks.

"They kept $100,000 and turned in only $57,000."

"They some dirty mutha-fuckas." Q says.

We meet Brick at the Wendy's on DuPont Highway.

"I know where the boy Jihad is staying for his curfews." Brick gives me some of the best news I heard in a long time.

"Where at, cuz?" I'm geeking to get back at the boy Jihad.

"He is staying out Chestnut Crossing apartments in Newark. He got to be in the house by 10 p.m." Brick tells us.

"What's the address?" Quincy asks Brick.

"It's 140-C, Chestnut Crossing Lane." He writes down the info on a napkin for us.

"See if you can find out something on that nigga, Kenji who be running around with Ronny." Q asks Brick.

"I got you. I'm about to send Umar some money. Are you adding to it?" Brick asks us.

We give Brick $200 a piece for Umar. I give him $200 for Littles and Cousin Gee, too.

Later on that night, Q and I are sitting in the laundry room out Chestnut Crossing Apartments. Jihad's apartment is directly across from where we lay and wait. It is 9:40 p.m. and he should be coming home any minute now. I don't have a mask on because I want him to see my face before I send him out of here. At 9:53 p.m., we hear the building's door open up.

Jihad says to whoever is waiting outside in the car, "Hold up, wait 'til I get in the crib."

I peek out into the hallway and see Jihad sticking his key into the door. I walk out with Q on my heels. Jihad quickly turns his head around to face me and I blow a kiss at him as I aim the Desert Eagle .50 Cal at his face.

"Boom!"

His whole face comes off and blood hits me in my face.

Quincy stands over top of him and shoots him four more times. I hear a woman yelling Jihad's name outside so I tell Q, "Let's bounce."

We run through the laundry room and escape out the building.

Chapter 20

Two weeks later in Atlanta, Georgia . . .

"Cuz, it's poppin down here in the A." Larue says to Big Tee, Ronny, and Kenji as they eat their meal at Ruby Tuesday's."

"Yeah, it's my second home. I got the trap doing numbers." Ronny boasts about his money making trap on the Westside of Atlanta.

"We needed a break for a minute from up the way. My mind ain't been right since my young boah Jihad got rocked."

Tee still can't believe he got caught slipping like that.

"It's all good cuz, you can chill for as long as you want." Ronny says.

"Yeah, I'll lay low down here that way D.B. and them will get relaxed thinking shit is sweet." Tee says.

"I'm cool with his homegirl, Dana. I seen her pushing one of the nigga's whips. I think he be over there chillin." Kenji says.

He is cool with a lot of females in the city. He is a shrewd manipulator that knows how to seem innocent to all the ladies. He is a huge asset to Ronny's crew.

"Where is the crib?" Tee asks.

"It's over by P.S." Kenji replies.

"We will start keeping an eye on the crib when we get back." Tee says.

The last month has been relatively quiet in the city. Things seem to be on the verge of normalcy. Promo sent 100 kilos of pure Columbian cocaine with the Mercedes Benz stamp on them. I hit Q off with twenty bricks. Brick got fifteen of them. Deen, Bay-Bay and Quadir got five apiece. The remaining fifty I sold to my folks in Philly and D.C. I haven't seen Big Tee or none of his boys in about a month. Brick says he heard they are down in Atlanta. That's cool with me. They can stay down there for all I care. I've been spending my time between Los Angeles, D.C. and Philly with my three chicks; Lauren, Kennidy and Khadijah.

I'm about to fall back from Lauren because I seen a picture in Hip Hop Weekly of her and Lil' Wayne all hugged up. The article said they are starting to become close. See, I don't care if niggas be fucking one of my side bitches, but I ain't sharing my main bitches. Plus, I got to cut her off because she doesn't fit into the proposition I laid on Khadijah and Kennidy last week. I remember that day clearly...

"Whose house is this?" Kennidy asks me when I parked in front of Khadijah's house in Philly.

"Chill out and come on." I answer as I get out my 650i BMW. I use my key to open the door. When we walk into the immaculately decorated house, I can see Kennidy is impressed with the décor.

"As-Salaamu-Alaikum!" I yell upstairs to Khadijah who I can hear walking around.

"Wa laikum-As-Salaam, are you alone?" She asks.

"Nah. Come here for a sec."

"Okay. Let me garb up first."

"You don't have to cover up." I tell her.

Khadijah walks into the living room and stops abruptly as she looks at me, then Kennidy, then finally at our fingers entwined together like a couple. She has on a pair of pink Juicy sweats and a white tank-top. I see Kennidy assessing the beautiful woman with long hair down to her back.

"What's going on Salaam?" Khadijah asks, skeptically.

I lead Kennidy to the couch and gesture for her to take a

seat. Then I wrap my arm around Khadijah's shoulders and pull her close, giving her a kiss on her cheek as I lead her to the love seat across from Kennidy. I go stand in front of the fireplace, then I began my spiel.

"Khadijah meet Kennidy. And Kennidy, this is Khadijah." I introduced my two favorite women to each other.

"Devon, what is this all about?" That was Kennidy.

"Yeah, what's up?" Khadijah asked.

"If you two chill, I will explain. Since you've known me, Khadijah, have I ever lied to you?" I look at Khadijah.

"No," she replied.

"Have I ever lied to you, Kennidy?"

"Not that I know of." Kennidy said.

"And, I will not start now. I'm a real nigga, so I gots to be real with both of you. Both of you mean a lot to me. I realize your worth as women. I want both of you to be a part of my life. I'm not going to leave you alone." I say, looking to Kennidy. I then look at Khadijah and continue, "I'm not leaving you alone, either. See, I'm a hell of a nigga. I can take care of both of you; physically, mentally, financially, and spiritually. And, I'm talking about marriage to make it official." I laid it on the table for them to consider.

"Wow." Kennidy said with her mouth open.

"Salaam, I know Allah says a Muslim man can have up to four wives but what makes you think I want to be a part of that?" Khadijah said to me.

"Both of you got brothers and male relatives. You see how they run around behind their girlfriend's or wives' backs with other women. I will not do that. You two are all I want and need. If either of you marry someone else, I guarantee you, they'll cheat on you." I broke it down to them.

"If they do, I'm gone." Kennidy responded.

"Plus, ain't no more niggas left like me. They are either dead or in jail. I'm trying to build families and empires with both of you." I walk and stand in between them while I look at them.

"No man has ever came at me like this. You are right there, ain't nobody like you for sure." Kennidy said.

Khadijah, who started pacing the living room floor said, "I love you, Salaam. With all of my heart and I want you to be my husband but I have to really think about this. How would you split your time between us?" She asked a valid question.

"I would stay with you three nights and Kennidy three nights. The other night, I'd stay at my condo, alone. I will take care of all of your bills and shopping sprees." I smiled because they both love to shop.

"Devon, I am leaning towards doing it. I can see Khadijah and I hanging out getting mani's and pedi's." Kennidy gave Khadijah a high-five. I'm glad the ice got broken easily between them.

"I am a patient man. I will wait for my two future wives." I said to them.

"Kennidy let me get your number so we can chat because I am digging those Loubs you got on." Khadijah grabbed her iPhone.

"Hey, Dijah, let me holla at you real quick before I leave." I said walking into the kitchen.

"My man Kareem is sending his sister over here later with $680,000. Count it for me to make sure it's straight. You can take $5000 for yourself." I told her.

Before we leave, Kennidy asked to use the bathroom. Then Khadijah sat on my lap and kissed me before she whispered in my ear, "I better be your number one?" I let out a chuckle.

Little did she know that Kennidy was and is number one in my heart.

That was a hell of a day....

*****

Two days Later. . .11:15 p.m.:

My cousin, Deen and I are sitting in the parking lot of Dunkin Doughnuts on Maryland Avenue, eating a dozen of doughnuts.

"How can a big fat guy like you only eat one doughnut? I ask as I laugh at him.

"Go 'head with that bullshit, cuz." Deen says.

129

"Man, you go to Burger King and order a Whopper Junior and shit." I clown him.

"You got jokes, huh cuz? Serious though cuz, my smut bitch down your way be fucking Ronny too and she said she is riding with me." Deen says.

"Who are you talking about?" I had to know who this bitch was.

"My bitch Jas." He tells me.

"I didn't know he was hittin Jasmin. Do you trust her?" I ask to see where his head is at.

"It don't matter because she outta here once we kill that nigga." He replies.

"Put that shit in motion. I will get my youngin, Allen to help us." I tell Deen.

"I am going to get on it, ASAP." Deen says.

*****

Three Nights Later. . .3:10 a.m.:

"Yes! Yes! Fuck me harder!" Jas screams as Ronny fucks her hard from behind.

"Take this dick, you dirty whore!" Ronny says, as he pulls her hair.

Jas gave Deen the house key earlier so we can gain entry easily. Drake was playin on the stereo, as we crept inside the bedroom where the porn stars were fucking like rabbits.

"Damn cuz, you got caught with your pants down, literally." I say, as I lay the .44 Bulldog to the back of Ronny's head.

"You slimy Bitch!" Was his only reply.

Deen yanks him out the bed onto the floor.

"Get dressed, Jas and wait in the living room." Deen tells his bitch.

"You know it's over, right?" I tell Ronny while I handcuff his hands behind his back.

"Come on, D.B., don't kill me. I got $100,000 for you if you let me go." Ronny tries to bargain.

"I don't want your money, I want your life." I duct tape his mouth and feet then we drag him to the living room. Allen had laid plastic down on the floor. Ronny is scared to death because he knows it's over for him. Deen leaves to drop Jasmin off over her sister's crib while Allen and me try to pressure Ronny into luring Big Tee over.

"Are you going to call Tee or what?" I ask Ronny.

I got the hot curling iron in my hand, waiting on his answer. When he shook his head no, I placed the hot iron on his naked back. His skin started to sizzle and he let out a muffled scream. I kicked him in the side of his face.

"Pussy, we can do this all day. I ain't got nowhere to be." I pistol-whipped him with the .44, causing blood to pour from the gashes in his head.

"Chill, big guy. You don't want to kill him until we get him to make the call first." Allen slurred, high off the Percs he downed an hour ago.

"Yeah, you are right." I say.

I go into the bathroom to wash blood off my face. I tell Allen to keep an eye on Ronny. While I'm cleaning myself up, I hear a loud crash like glass breaking. I run out into the living room, gun in hand. I see no sign of Ronny and I see the living room window busted open. Allen is on the porch looking down the street. I go to see what has his attention and I see a butt-naked, handcuffed Ronny running full speed down the street.

"What the fuck happened?" I yell at this stupid nigga.

"I must've nodded off. Then I heard a window break and by the time I knew what was going on, that nigga was gone." He gave up a bullshit excuse.

"Mutha-fucka you let that nigga get away. We will probably never see him again." I say, pissed at this nigga.

"My bad homie. I fucked up." He puts his head down in shame.

"Fuck! Yo, clean that glass up while I wrap the plastic up and grab the niggas clothes. We got to get the fuck out of this house just in case he tells the cops."

I race into the house to straighten up.

Chapter 21

Wilmington's FBI Field Office...10 a.m.:

"I will be turning the reigns over to Special Agent John Taylor of the FBI's Baltimore Field Office. He will update you on what steps will be taken to bring down the murderous group of thugs known as the Devon Baker Gang. It's all yours, Agent Taylor." Special Agent Kelly said as he steps away from the podium.

"Good morning, I am Special Agent John Taylor from the FBI's Baltimore Division. My team of four agents and an agent from the ATF have been summoned by the U.S. District Attorney, Eric Holder, to head the investigation of Devon Baker and his band of gun-toting associates. I know that everyone here is aware of some of the alleged crimes committed by this group. From my intel we have here, we have somewhat of an idea of who the players are." He points to the projector screen by him. "This here is the brain behind the organization, Devon Baker, age 36. He just completed a twelve year federal sentence and with his extensive record, any more convictions will lay him down for life. He is extremely dangerous. He is a suspect in at least six recent murders and three from the 1990's. This serious-looking fella is his second in command, William Holiday a.k.a. Umar. We have him currently on ice at Federal Detention Center in Philadelphia, on a weapons charge and money laundering. We think he is our ticket to bring the gang down if we can scare him with a twenty year sentence." Agent Taylor lays down his game plan of getting Umar to snitch on his crew.

A female agent raises her hand to speak, "Don't you think that will be difficult because of the street code of silence these guys live by? I mean, it is alleged they murdered two federal informants." She says holding up two fingers.

"Yes, it will be difficult, but it's an avenue worth trying. Ok, this here is Kenneth Whitby a.k.a. Brick. He is the laid back one out of the bunch, but don't let the laid back demeanor fool you. This guy has tricked many men out of their lives. This character here, his name is Quincy Dorsett. He just came home from doing a five-year sentence and has already been linked to four homicides. He moves a lot of the gang's narcotics. These two fellas right here also move a lot of the gang's narcotics. On the left is Ernest Morris a.k.a. Bay-Bay and on the right is Harold Covington a.k.a. Skully. Mr. Covington loves the ladies and our intel leads me to believe we may be able to use an undercover female agent to get close to him. I hear he loves to pillow talk. Next, we have the young guns of the gang. These three, along with the four deceased young men in the bottom of the screen, sole job is to kill. They take their orders from Baker. The baby-faced assassin in the middle is, Allen Cenitez. He is a suspect in at least ten murders. To his right, Gary Collins a.k.a. Cousin Gee; this young one makes Wayne Perry look like a choir boy. He is currently on a probation violation. Finally, we have, Lamont Wisher a.k.a. Littles. He, right now, is in prison for the shooting at a skating rink. We have sister cases ongoing with Devon Baker's relatives, Deen Baker, Vance Baker, Darnell Lyons, Darius Lyons, and Samuel Bowman. We will try to intertwine these cases together. From our estimates, these individuals distribute 100 kilos of cocaine and 1000 pounds of marijuana per month. Our goal will be to charge them with the RICO, CCE 848 Kingpin, Drug Conspiracy, Murder, Weapon Possession, and Money Laundering. If we work together, we will be able to eradicate these dangerous individuals from the streets of Wilmington. I will now let Detective Sullivan, give you all a more in-depth look into the gang. Thank you." Agent Taylor finally finishes, leaving the floor for the dirty detective.

Sullivan approaches the podium to speak but his mind was elsewhere because the hammer was about to come down on D.B. and he needed to warn him.

Chapter 22

A few days later – Jummu'ah Friday...12:01 p.m.:

"Come on, D.B.! We are going to be late." Bay-Bay yells from the living room in Dana's house.

"Yeah Abdus Salaam, We got to get there fast because Hasa Somali is giving the khutbah and he brings a crowd." Khadijah says.

"I'm coming now. Let me put some Egyptian Musk on real quick." I tell them.

We are on our way up Philly for Jummu'ah. I grab my .45 and tuck it in my jeans under my throbe before we walk out. Bay-Bay is leading the way, followed by Khadijah, then me.

"Hey, Bay, are you driving?" I ask Bay-Bay.

"Nah, Khadijah got it." He says as he turns around to hand Khadijah his car keys. I finished locking the house door and when I turned back around, death was upon us.

"Boc! Boc! Boc! Boc! Pop! Pop! Pop! Pop! Boc! Pop! Pop! Boc! Pop! Pop! Bo! Boc! Pop!"

A Toyota Camry pulls up in front of the house as the driver and passenger rained bullets on us. I could not even reach for my pistol because of the rapid fire of their guns. I dive face first through the patio window to avoid being shot. Once I heard the shooting stop and them burning rubber outta there, I peek my head up to survey my surroundings. I ignore the blood leaking from my forehead as I rush out to Khadijah and Bay-Bay. Khadijah's green hijab is soaked in blood that's seeping from the bullet wound in her chest. She is trying to tell me something but she's choking on blood coming out of her mouth. I take my Kufi off to press it against the wound. Dana's nosey next door neighbor is now standing next to me.

"Please call an ambulance! Please! I yell to the neighbor.

I run over to Bay-Bay and turn him over on his back. My lifelong friend has four holes in his chest area and one in his forehead. He is no longer with us. I sigh then close his eyes and make dua for him. I quickly bury my gun in Dana's garden once I hear the police sirens. I lay Khadijah's head in my lap as I attempt to apply enough pressure to stop the bleeding. The paramedics and police rush to the scene. When I move out the way so the paramedics could work on Khadijah, I watch as she takes her last breath. . .

To live and die in the most dangerous city in America....

*****

Losing two of my dearest friends on account of something that had to do with me was very hard to deal with. There was nothing I could have done to prevent it, either. We had the Janaza prayer for Bay-Bay the next day and buried him up Chester, PA next to our other friend, Go-Go. Khadijah's Janaza was a day after Bay-Bay's. Her family is big with most of the males entrenched in the streets, so it was a no-brainer they wanted blood. I explain to her brothers and uncles what was going on, so now I have the notorious Bey family ready to put in work.

*****

A week later. . .4:20 p.m.:

Quincy, Brick and I are over Umar's house, talking to his girl Elise who just came from visiting Umar at FDC.

"D.B., he says that they want you bad and they offered to give him immunity if he go to the Grand Jury to testify." Elise says.

"What else he say?" I ask her.

"He said, they know a lot, but they need someone to stamp their allegations. He says to tell all of you to leave the country before it's too late.

"I'm going to bounce, but I ain't leaving until I handle them niggas, first." I say.

We give Elise $3,000 for her and the kids, then we head on out. We stop at a stash house Q has in Collins Park out in New Castle so we can chill for a few hours before we go searching for Big Tee and his squad.

"The dickhead, Sullivan told me they got the feds from B-more up here working to build a case against us. They calling us the Devon Baker Gang." I laugh once I tell them that one.

"Stop playin, man." Q says in disbelief.

"Walahi! He says they got profiles on all of us." I say.

"Me too?" Brick asks like he ain't got his hands dirty.

"Yeah nigga, you too!" I tell him

"Shit man, we need to get out of here like Umar said." Brick says.

"I ain't rollin until I get at least one of them for what they did to Khadijah and Bay-Bay." I say as thoughts of that fateful day flash in my mind.

We smoke a few blunts while we watch 'Paid in Full' on DVD. Brick says he's about to take his young girl to Atlantic City for the night. I'm going down D.C. to fuck with Kennidy for a few days. Q says he got to stop pass Valerie's crib before he go up Philly. We all promise to check in once we get to our destinations.

Quincy pulls up behind Valerie's house on the Westside. He holds his P-95 Ruger in his hand as he exits his rental. He can't afford to be slipping this late in the game. He uses his key to the back door and enters the quiet house. When he walks through the kitchen, into the living room, he sees Valerie watching Atlanta housewives while laying her head in a sleeping Kenji's lap.

"Why you got this clown ass nigga over here?" Q barks loud, awaking Kenji and startling Valerie.

"Please, Quincy, put the gun up! Please don't shoot him!" She stares wide-eyed at the Ruger in Q's hand.

"Chill the fuck out, Valerie! This ain't got nothing to do with you." Q yells.

"What's going on, Q? You and me ain't got no beef." Kenji tries to explain.

"Nigga, you runnin around with Ronny and them. You know what's up!"

Q points the gun at Kenji, who puts his hands up to block his face. "Don't shoot me man! A scared Kenji pleas.

"Q, don't shoot him! Please! For me!" Valerie says, tearfully.

Not paying his homegirl any attention, Q pumps two bullets in Kenji's head, spilling his brains all over the wall.

"Aaahhhhhhhh!" Valerie screams as she scurries into the corner.

"Shhhhh. Come here Valerie. It's going to be ok." Q says to her as he hugs her trembling body.

"Why Q?" She asks.

"He was the enemy. Go grab some towels and a blanket." He says while directing her to walk in front of him.

Sometimes in life, people do things that they live to regret. When Quincy shot Valerie in the back of her head, he knew he would regret this for the rest of his life.

Chapter 23

"Damn Q, why did you knock Valerie off, man?" I ask Quincy while we waited on our food at Cracker Barrel, over the bridge in New Jersey.

A sad look encompasses his face. "I had to, man. She was buggin after I murked that nigga," he says with regret.

"She didn't know the nigga was with them, but broads got to really be careful about niggas they choose to fuck with." I say.

I wish Valerie could've been spared, but Quincy couldn't take the chance of her telling everybody or even going to the cops.

"Yo, man that shit has been bothering me for real. I had to do it D.B." He sounds torn up inside.

"Ask Allah to forgive you Ahki." I say to him.

Meanwhile on the Westside, Flame is standing on 5th Street talking to Boobie and Slone, unaware of death lurking. Allen is across the street in the ally, masked up and holding a tech-9. He places a call to the big Homie.

"Hey, I'm on 5th and the basketball nigga out here. What do you want me to do?" Allen asks.

"Nah, let him slide. He's Muslim." D.B. states, saving Flame's life.

"Solid, solid. He lucky, cuz." Allen says.

I am supposed to go see my P.O. today for my monthly visit. However, I don't plan on seeing him no more after he pulled that stunt the last visit. *Catch me if you can, 'cause I'm the Gingerbread Man. Or Fritz Ward, as my fake driver's license says that I am carrying.* I paid $1200 for the official joint. I'm cruising in the Ford Flex rental out Greenville, sightseeing all the million dollar mansions. I'm thinking about how my life ended up like this so fast. One minute, I had everything a man could want. Money, beautiful women, jewels, cars, lavish condo, etc…Then, it all gets turned upside down. Niggas want to see me dead and the police want me in a jail cell. I'm going to murder these niggas and then I'm packing my shit and heading for Italy. My family will have to visit me there. I'm going to ask Kennidy to relocate with me and be my wife. The two million I have stashed will last a lifetime in Italy.

*****

Three days later - Washington, D.C...6:21 p.m.:

"I'm outta here soon, Kennidy. I plan on never coming back to this country." I say to Kennidy, while we eat our dinner at Carmine's Italian restaurant on 7th Street.

"What? Why? What about us?" She drops her fork and stares at me for answers.

"I ain't trying to go back to prison. The Feds are on my line and I don't want to get gunned down in these streets." I say.

"So it's just fuck me huh?" She asks me.

"No, baby. I want you to come with me. I can't picture life without you. I have enough money to last us a lifetime since the cost of living where we would live is so cheap. Please come with me." I grab hold of both her hands.

"Where?"

"Italy," I say.

"Devon, anywhere you will lead me, I will follow. I trust you and you are my best friend in the entire world." Kennidy tells me.

"I love you Kennidy, with all of my heart."

"I love you Devon...more than Coretta loved Martin. More than Jada loves Will. More than Michelle loves Barack. More than Wilma loves Fred. Damn, are you gonna tell me to stop?"

140

She says, causing us both to laugh.

*****

Two weeks later – Riverside Projects...9:10 p.m.:

Larue is desperately on the lookout trying to find some loud pack. He got the young girl, Camille waiting for him at the Best Western. He pulls up to Meatball, who is standing on 27th and Bowers Street.

"What up, Naafi? Who got the loud?" Larue asks Naafi with the dark tint only slightly cracked in the Chevy Malibu.

"Who dat?" Naafi tries to get a better view to see who is in the car.

"It's me, Larue." He says, rolling the window down.

Naafi sees the young nigga who shot his boy, D.B. and he goes right into his Oscar-winning performance. See, a lot of people don't know that Naafi and D.B. are good friends because they are from different hoods. They got cool through Kennidy and D.B. made sure Naafi was cool during his Fed time. Pictures, money, books, were the norm.

"I got that White Widow and Headband. Take me to my aunt's crib around the corner." Naafi says, as he gets in the passenger seat. He is conscious enough to grab the door with his hoodie sleeve as to not leave any prints.

"Is that shit fire?" Larue asks.

"Yeah, nigga. Make a right here and make a right on the last block." Naafi instructs him to go on the back block by Parina Chow.

When they park, Larue hands Naafi $50 for 3.5 grams. Naafi stuffs the money in his pocket.

Before he gets out the car, he asks Larue, "You still beefin with that nigga, D.B.?"

"Yeah. The nigga hiding but I'm gonna catch his ass." Larue says.

"No you're not." Naafi says as he whips out the .10mm and squeezes the trigger.

"Boc! Boc! Boc! Boc! Boc! Boc! Boc!"

Naafi searches Larue for the gun he knows he is carrying.

He finds a pretty Glock .40 in his waistband. He quickly exits the car and disappears between the houses. Once he makes it to his people's crib on 24th and Pine Street, he makes a call.

"D.B., As-Salaamu-Alaikum."

"Walaikum As-Salaam. What up, Naf?" I greet.

"Make sure you treat my girl, Kennidy right." Naafi states.

"Is that why you called, cuz?" I chuckle at this crazy nigga.

"Read the paper tomorrow. It was a big upset in the NBA tonight." Naafi tells me.

"Did Lebron and them lose?" I ask. "Just call me in the a.m., Insha'Allah." He says and hangs up.

Chapter 24

To say I was elated when I read about Larue being found murdered in a car in Riverside Projects, would be an understatement. I owe Naafi big time for removing that problem out of my life. All these months of trying to get this nigga was stressful. They say his funeral was crowded. I heard that Ronny and Big Tee were in attendance.

I told Primo to send 100 bricks and he came through like always. Brick, Deen, Q and I are going to get ghost once we finish this last package. Brick is going down Texas to fuck with Markie Gold's old Mexican plug. Deen is relocating to Pittsburgh. Quincy is going down to Jamaica and I'm bouncing to Italy with Kennidy. I gave Sullivan $350,000 to "lock" Ronny and Tee up and deliver them to me. I'm trying to get this shit over with.

We are over Quincy's cousin's apartment which is one of our stash houses. My brother is there to guard the bricks with his life. I'm on my phones talking to my peoples who are putting their orders in for the fish scale cocaine. Quincy has left and came back two times with bags of money. He is moving them birds like a true "Bird Boss."

"Yo, I got a sale down Dover tomorrow for one key and four and half ounces." Q tells me his plans for tomorrow.

"Who are the dudes? I ask.

"Some Dover niggas I was locked up with. My man Tims is going with me. He knows them dudes." Q says.

"You want me to go with you?" I ask.

"Nah, I'm good." He states.

"Make sure you take your hammer." I say, pointing to our two guns that are laying on the table.

"Oh, you know I am." He says as he mistakenly grabs my .40 Cal off the table. I grab his .45 and tuck it in my waistband.

"Hey, make sure you call me before you leave and when you finish." I tell Q as I prepare to leave.

"Ok. As-Salaamu Alaikum."

"Walaikum As-Salaam." I salaam my man for the last time.

*****

The Next Day...2:20 p.m.:

"D.B., I'm hungry. Can you bring me some Burger King and some blunts?" My brother asks me. He is guarding the bricks so we got to bring him his food.

"Call Q because I'm on my way up Philly." I tell him.

"I called him three times, but he ain't answering." He says.

"Let me try calling him. I'll call you back." I say as I dial Q on my other phone. He didn't answer none of my calls. He should've been back from Dover by now. My cousin Darius calls me.

"Hey, Cuddy! Have you talked to Q?"

"Nah, I'm looking for him myself. He went down Dover to take care of something but he should've been back." I tell my cousin.

"Tell him to call me when you catch him." Cuz says before he hangs up.

I call Brick to ask did he hear from Q but he told me no. A few minutes later, my cousin Deen calls me.

"Cuz, they shot Q! And it's bad."

"Who shot him? Where?" I ask, shocked at the news.

"Them clown ass Dover niggas shot and robbed him." He says.

"Man, fuck!" I yell into the phone.

"Why did he go down there to fuck with them?" Deen asks.

"Yo, how did you find out?" I asked.

"The boah Tims that was with him called me. He is

144

supposed to meet me when he gets back up here." Deen says.

"I want to talk to that nigga, too. I'm on my way to get you. Where are you?" I ask him.

"Come get me at my mom's house." Deen informs me. As I make my way back to Delaware, I make dua for Q and I shed a single tear. This nigga Tims got a lot of explaining to do about what the fuck happened. If he sounds suspect, I'm blowing his face off.

Deen and I are on our way to meet this nigga Tims, so he can give us the run down on what happened to Quincy. We are meeting him on the Hill-Top at Canby's Pool; I guess he wants to meet in a public place to be safe.

"Cuz, if what he saying don't sound right, I'm bangin him." I inform Deen.

"Nah, cuz. Let's see what's up first." Deen replies. "I'm telling you, he was in on that shit. Why didn't they shoot him, too?" I ask the million dollar question.

"I don't know cuz." Deen answers.

I call out to the hospital to get an update on Q. I'm told by Losha that he is in critical condition. It pains me that I can't go out to the hospital to see my homeboy because I am on the run for probation violation.

We park our car two blocks away, just in case shit gets messy, so nobody can identify the getaway vehicle. Once we reach the front entrance of the pool, I didn't see Tims anywhere in sight. I was beginning to think he got cold feet at the last minute. The pool was closed but it was a softball game being played across on the field. It was a few people littering the park. A few minutes later, Tims approaches us, but I don't see exactly where he comes from. We all speak, then I ask him his version of what happened to Q and the story doesn't make sense to me.

"So, you were walking in front of Q, then you said the niggas came from the back and just started shooting at Q, but they never shot at you, right?" I ask him because it doesn't make sense to just shoot Q and leave Tims there as a witness or let Tims get a chance to fire on them.

"Yeah, I-I-I don't know why but they did." Tims says nervously.

"So they just grabbed the money and ran? What were you doing the entire time?" I asked.

"Yeah, they grabbed the money and jetted. I was standing there, shook," he responded.

"Do you know where them niggas live at?" Deen asks him.

"Yeah," he says.

"You are taking us down there tonight so we can get at them." Deen orders.

"Yo, where's the gun Q had on him?" I ask that nigga.

"He didn't have a hammer on him that I know of." He lies.

Wrong answer nigga. He never leaves the house without his gun on him. Plus, I know he had my .40 Cal on him.

"How many shooters was it?" Deen asks.

"It was two shoo-"

"Boc! Boc! Boc!" I hit him three times; all chest shots then he fell to the ground.

"What the fuck, cuz!" Deen yells as he looks down at Tims' lifeless body.

"Fuck that nigga! He was down with that shit!" I say as we quickly walk away.

Once we get into the car and pull off, Deen starts it again,

"We needed that nigga to show us where them niggas be at. You should of waited cuz."

"Nah, once he would of left we would've never seen him again. We can get Scabby to get info on them niggas since he lives down Dover." I explain to Deen.

"I got a few dudes down there I can ask to check on it for us." Deen says.

*****

A Few Days Later...3:15 p.m.:

I am down D.C., chillin with Kennidy at her house. Days have been long and gloomy for all of us as we pray for Quincy's recovery. When I hear my phone ringing and see that it's Brick calling, I knew it wasn't any good news.

"Hello." I answer.

146

"He-he-he gone man. He's gone." Brick cries into the phone.

The worst pain I ever felt in my life engulfs me. I feel the tears about to come. "Let me call you back." I hang up the phone and fall to my knees in tears.

Kennidy comes running to console me. Losing my man Q was unbearable. As the news of Quincy's death spread, I began getting phone calls from everyone. I didn't feel like talking to a lot of people, so I told Kennidy to answer my calls for me.

Quincy's mom told me that the police will not be releasing Q's body for a couple more days, so we had to put off the Janazah. Skully and I went to get the white shroud (sheets), sponges, soap, buckets, oils, and camphor; all needed to wash and wrap the body for burial. I gave Q ten bricks, but it was only five that he had left at the stash house. That meant it was some money to be collected, but I didn't know from whom, though.

*****

Two Nights Later...11:19 p.m.:

I get a text from the dirty cop, Sullivan telling me to meet him down Brandywine Park and to bring his $350,000. He must of grabbed them niggas up. I ain't just gonna walk into a double cross, so I take precaution. I dress in all black with my police-issued bullet proof vest on under my thermal. I also wear my bullet-proof fitted baseball cap. I am taking Allen with me, just in case I need backup. I pack my twin .357 snub noses.

When I pull up in Brandywine, all I see is total darkness. I'm in a black X-5 BMW with dark tinted windows. Allen is laying across the back seat, clutching a Mac 11. As I drive closer towards the river, I can see Sullivan leaving his car. I get out the X-5 clutching the Nike gym bag, containing $350,000 in my left hand and my .357 in my right.

"What do you have for me, copper?" I say to him as I drop the bag next to his feet.

"D.B., I always keep my word." He says.

"Come on, let's get this over with." I tell him.

He opens the car door and yanks a handcuffed Ronny out. He slams Ronny to the ground.

"Ronny meet the Grim Reaper." Sullivan says.

"Fuck you! Fuck D.B.! Yall can suck my dick! Ronny spits with venom." I admit, he is going out like a trooper. "Take the money and get out of here copper." I tell Sullivan.

"Have fun you two." He says before he picks up the bag of money, gets in his car and drives off.

"Did you really think I was a washed-out old head?" I asked Ronny.

"Suck my dick!" He yells. Allen gets out and walks over to us.

"Go 'head, punish the nigga, D.B." Allen says.

"Since you going out like a trooper, I'm going to give you a soldier's death." I turn him over on his back and hand Allen one of my .357s. I aim at his face and let my rage go. Allen follows my lead.

"Pow! Pow! Pow! Pow! Pow! Pow! Pow! Pow! Pow! Pow! Pow! Pow!"

To live and die in the most dangerous city in America....

Chapter 25

Muslim Cemetery – Chester, PA. . .

We arrive at the burial site to lay to rest one of the realest niggas ever to live. Muslims from every side of the city came to send Q off. We took out the casket and laid Q in the grave. Muslims don't get buried in caskets. I made dua for my comrade, then picked up three handfuls of dirt and threw on top of him. Then I grabbed a shovel and started throwing dirt on the body in order to fill the grave. Manny, Malik, Skully, Shawn Truitt, Big Oak, and a few other brothers, assisted in filling the grave with dirt. While shoveling the dirt, I contemplated my next moves which would be to move the remaining ninety bricks, find this nigga, Big Tee, and then take off to Italy.

*****

The Next Day - Washington, D.C. . .7:01 p.m.:

Kennidy and I are at the Wizards vs. Cavaliers game at the Verizon Center.

"I'm here for you in any way you need me while you deal with the loss of your friend." Kennidy says to me, while we stand at the concession stand during halftime.

"Thank you for the support, Kennidy. This has been a wake-up call for me. We can't duck death when it's our time to go." I say.

"I know. That's why we got to live right before the Lord.

You should be aiming to make it to Heaven." She sincerely says to me.

"I got to get my soul right before it's too late." I say.

"We all do Devon."

I change the subject because talk like that is souring my mood.

"I am taking you to New York this weekend on a shopping spree." I tell her, hoping to make her smile.

"For real, Devon?"

"Yeah. We taking $5,000 apiece. Is that enough for you?" I ask her. "That's more than enough." She is smiling from ear to ear.

*****

The Next Day – Wilmington...12:30 p.m.:

I'm driving down Claymont Street near Leroy's bar when a gold Honda Accord cruises by slowly. *Hold up! I know my eyes ain't deceiving me. Was that Big Tee?* I stop to look in my rear view mirror. The Honda stops as well. I pull over to park as the driver in the Honda does the same. I get out my car with my .9mm with a 30-shot ladder and extra clip. The driver of the Honda stands in the middle of the street with a .40 cal at his side. I know Big Tee from any distance.

"Boc! Boc! Boc!" I let loose on him.

He ducks behind a car and returns fire.

"Pop! Pop!" I get low and make my way towards him.

"Boc! Boc! Boc! Boc! Boc! Boc!" I tear the car up he his hiding behind, forcing him to hide behind another car.

"Pop! Pop! Pop! Pop!" He causes me to dive on the ground as his bullets hit the house behind me.

He gets up, shooting to kill, "Pop! Pop! Pop!"

He has me pinned down, but I'm counting his bullets. That .40 cal only holds twelve bullets. I reach the gun over the car hood and fire, just to back him up.

"Boc! Boc! Boc!" I look up to see him kneeling between two cars. I got plenty of bullets left, so I shoot a barrage at him.

"Boc! Boc! Boc! Boc! Boc! Boc! Boc! Boc! Boc!" This must've let him know I got a thirty because he tried to make a

dash back to his car. He shoots blindly over his shoulder.
"Pop! Pop! Pop! Click!"
Twelve shots and he knows he's doomed. I start chasing behind him.
"Boc! Boc! Boc!
I hit him in the leg causing him to fall to the ground. I make my way over to him as he tries to crawl away. I am standing over top of him with my gun aimed at his face as we lock eyes. Before I can pull the trigger to end his life and this war, my mind went back in time; to a time when the entire Westside was one big family. A time when Big Tee came up idolizing me and my crew. A time when I watched him make a name for himself. A time when we were friends. I thought of Q, Bay-Bay, Ricky, O, and Pac. All lost in this war. I think of all the lives I took. This shit has to end now.

"It's over cuz. I don't want no more beef. You owe me that for letting you live." I lower my gun.

"Thanks, D.B.," he says. I run to my car at the sounds of sirens.

I make my way to my homegirl Dana's crib so I can shower and change clothes. I'm going up to Philly for the day, once I holla at my Pops. Once my pops arrives at Dana's, we jump in her car and ride off.

"Don't look back, but I think that's the Feds behind us in that Cherokee." I tell my Pop.

"Shit! Are you dirty?" He asks nervously.

"Nah. I'm going to turn into Home Depot's parking lot and if they turn too, I'm running them." I let him know the plan.

I make the turn into Home Depot's parking lot and the Cherokee does the same thing. I bust a quick U-turn and accelerate out of there. The Cherokee gives chase. I see an Impala join in the chase as well. I roar down 38th Street then make a right at Van Buren Street. More cars fly by me going in the opposite direction until they spot my car. My Pops is scared to death.

"Don't kill us boy." He says.

"I got to call Brick to tell him to meet me somewhere. I call him to tell him that I am being chased by the Feds and to meet me at Quadir's grandmother's house on 30th. I got to shake these mutha fuckas. I turn left on 34th Street, then right onto Madison.

"I'm about to jump out and run." I tell my Pop.

"What? I can't run, man." He replies.

"They don't want you. Just chill." I reassure him to calm his nerves. As I near Quadir's grandma's house, I see fed cars coming up every street. When I get to 31st and Madison, I open my door to jump out as the car is slowing to a stop. The Feds got their guns drawn as they surround me.

"Hands up! Hands up! Put your fuckin hands where I can see them!" Yell the gun-toting agents.

I do as they say and surrender my freedom instead of my life. They handcuff us after a thorough pat down and place me in the back of the Cherokee. I see Brick and Quadir in the crowd of onlookers. I almost made it. The door to the Cherokee opens and I am face-to-face with agent John Taylor and some ATF broad.

"You are one elusive guy." Agent Taylor says to me.

"Do you want to tell us about all of the murders?" The ATF broad says.

I just look at her. She whispers something to Agent Taylor, I couldn't hear.

Then she asks, "Who killed your friend Quincy?" I say nothing at all, which infuriates her more.

"Do you want to help yourself? This is your last chance." She warns me.

I just shake my head no. Remaining silent.

"You're an asshole!" She yells then slams the door in my face.

Epilogue

Federal Courthouse – Wilmington, DE...9:30 a.m.:

In the Judge's Chamber before my violation of probation hearing, Federal Agent Taylor tries to persuade District Attorney Oberly and Judge Sleet to see things his way, while my attorneys, Joe Benson and Latoya Akemi, argue my innocence.

"Your Honor, Devon Baker is responsible for over twenty-five murders. At least ten he committed with his own hands. Also, the drugs flowing into this city can be attributed directly to Baker and his crew. We have to keep this dangerous felon off the streets, sir." Agent Taylor is trying to get the Judge to hold me in prison until he can build a case against me.

"Agent Taylor, I can't allow you to throw false allegations on my client. Your Honor, my client has been an asset to his community and Pastor Derrick Johnson is here today to attest to this. My client has held full-time employment since he was released from prison last year. He has been an exemplary citizen. His only fault was not keeping three appointments with his probation officer, which is the reason we are here today." Benson defends.

"Agent Taylor, I agree with Mr. Benson. We are here for a probation violation. I gave you permission to wiretap Mr. Baker's cellphones and cars. All intercepts have turned up nothing. Your informants proved to be unreliable. By law, I can't just make up crimes to charge Baker. I am only seeking twelve months for absconding. That's all I can do." District Attorney Oberly says.

"You are all making a big mistake. That man is a vicious killer." Agent Taylor says.

"Agent Taylor that is enough! No more allegations without proof. We are here for a violation of probation, not a criminal trial." Judge Sleet said with authority.

*****

Twenty minutes later...9:50 a.m.:

"Devon, That FBI guy has a real hard-on for you, I tell you. He is making you out to be worse than Charles Manson." My lawyer Benson tells me.

"Fuck him! So, what does the prosecutor recommend?" I ask.

"He is only asking for twelve months. Your charge only carries 7-13 months. Of course I am going to argue for seven months. I tell you, you're getting a second chance to change your life around. You got a beautiful girlfriend in D.C. waiting on you. You're smart. Hell, you got plenty of money. By the way, I can use a nice cash gift one of these days. Anyway, when you get out, just kiss Delaware goodbye and make D.C. your home. You don't need this shit." Benson sincerely advises me.

Latoya Akemi is just sitting there staring daggers at me. She is still angry with me because I ended our relationship. I stopped dealing with all my women so I could commit myself to Kennidy, the love of my life.

"Thanks for the advice Joe. I am definitely heading for D.C. when I get out. Let's go get this shit over with." I tell them.

After my P.O. spoke about my missed appointments and me getting shot, Pastor D. told the judge about me mentoring the youth in a few of his programs. He said he would like me to relocate to D.C. so I can help with his Re-entry Program. This caught the judge's attention; I saw the way he nodded his head in agreement. The prosecutor didn't really try to screw me around. He asked for a sentence of twelve months. I gave my best redemption of a changed man. You know...the same speech all criminals say when they stand before a judge. Now, it was Judge Sleet's turn to hand down his sentence.

"Mr. Baker, this is a difficult decision I'm faced to make today. I never seen, in all my years on this bench, as much of a vested interest in a violation of probation hearing. On one side, I have a decorated government agent levying horrible allegations against you and on the other side; we have a respectable pillar of the community, Pastor Johnson and your attorney, Mr. Benson, presenting all that you have done well over the last year. I am aware of the gun violence that is plaguing our city's streets. You, yourself, were a victim of this violence. I see that you are a very intelligent young man. However, I don't know if you are the solution to what's going on in our city or if you are part of the problem? So, I am going to sentence you to twenty-four months of imprisonment."

"What?" I inadvertently shout out.

Judge Sleet continues, "Wait, Wait, Mr. Baker. I could give you three more years of supervised release on top of the twenty-four months, but I am terminating all supervised probation after you complete your twenty-four month sentence. That way, you can go on with your life as you please. Mr. Baker, I wish you well in your future endeavors."

After surviving a bloody drug war that took the lives of over twenty individuals and having the city of Wilmington under siege, a two year sentence is a blessing. Allah has shown mercy on me again. In Chapter 55 Ar-Rahman, in the Noble Qu'ran, it says, "Then, which of the blesssings of Your Lord will you both deny?" I plan on marrying Kennidy when I get out of prison. I also plan on opening my own commercial cleaning company. Insha'Allah.

*****

Two Days Later – F.D.C. – Philadelphia, PA...1:05 p.m.:

Kennidy and my mom came to visit me before they ship me off to some federal prison located up in the mountains.

"Devon, two years is not too bad and you will have no probation either." Kennidy says while holding my hands as we sit in the visiting hall of FDC.

"Yeah, I know, but I would have rather gotten seven months." I reply.

"At least you are still alive. I would rather come visit you in jail, than visit your grave." Kennidy says.

"I feel you, babe. So, are you going to hold me down my entire bid?" I ask her.

"Yes."

"I mean, be 100 percent faithful and keep that pussy to yourself?" *I ain't with that sharing my chick shit.*

"Yes, Devon!" Kennidy tells me how much I mean to her, "I don't want anybody else but you. You do it for me."

"Kennidy, I want us to get married on the island of St. Thomas then have the most grand reception ever back in D.C. Money ain't a problem, so you can go all out." I tell her.

"Are you asking me to marry you, Devon?" She asks as she waves her ringless fingers in front of my face. Kennidy didn't notice my mom slip me the ring before she got up to use the restroom. In my hand, I possess a three and a half carat VS1 Diamond engagement ring that my jeweler Avi and I designed.

I had it made way back when I first came home, before I even had sex with anyone. I told Avi that one day I would give it to the woman most worthy, when he questioned why I was spending $32,000 on a ring when I had nobody to give it to at the time. Now, I found that somebody. When I grabbed Kennidy's hand and slid the sparkling ring onto her finger, her facial expression was one I wish Picasso could of painted.

"Kennidy will you complete my life by becoming my wife?"

"Yes Devon! Oh my God! Yes!" She starts crying and kissing me all over my face.

"The day I was born into this world is the day I want to marry you." I tell her.

"I can't wait to be Mrs. Kennidy Baker." She says, while staring at her ring.

"I got one more surprise for you. I can't make it to New York for our shopping spree, but you can still go. My mom got the $5,000 for you in the car." I love spoiling this woman.

"Oh Devon! Thank you! Thank you!" You are the best. I love you so much." Kennidy tells me.

"Kennidy, there are only two types of people in this world. Those who watch things happen and those who make things happen. I make things happen."

The End.

So Real You Feel You've Lived It!

Street Knowledge Publishing LLC
1902-B Maryland Ave
Wilmington, DE 19805
TOLL FREE:1.888.401.1114
www.streetknowledgepublishing.com

Date: _____

Purchaser _____

Mailing Address _____

City_____**State**_____**Zip Code**_____

Qty.	ISB Number	Title of Book	Price Each	Total
	978-0-9822515-6-0	Bloody Money	$15.00	
	978-0-9822515-9-1	Bloody Money 2	$15.00	
	978-0-9799556-4-8	Bloody Money 3	$15.00	
	978-0-9799556-0-0	Tommy Good Story	$15.00	
	978-0-9822515-0-8	Tommy Good Story II	$15.00	
	978-0-9746199-1-0	Me & My Girls	$15.00	
	978-0-9746199-0-3	Cash Ave	$15.00	
	978-0-9822515-1-5	Merry F$$kin' Xmas	$15.00	
	978-0-9799556-1-7	A Day After Forever	$15.00	
	978-0-9822515-3-9	A Day After Forever 2	$15.00	
	978-0-9746199-6-5	Don't Mix the Bitter with the Sweet	$15.00	
	978-0-9799556-9-3	Playing For Keeps	$15.00	
	978-0-9799556-3-1	Pain Freak	$15.00	
	978-0-9799556-5-5	Dipped Up	$15.00	
	978-0-9799556-6-2	No Love No Pain	$15.00	
	978-0-9746199-4-1	Dopesick	$15.00	
	978-0-9799556-7-9	Lust, Love & Lies	$15.00	
	978-0-9746199-7-2	The Queen Of New York	$15.00	
	978-0-9799556-5-5	Dipped Up	$15.00	
	978-0-9746199-8-9	Sin 4 Life	$15.00	
	978-0-9822515-4-6	A Little More Sin	$15.00	
	978-0-9746199-5-8	The Hunger	$15.00	
	978-09746199-3-4	Money Grip	$15.00	
	978-0-9822515-7-7	Young Rich & Dangerous	$15.00	
	978-0-9822515-7-7	Young Rich & Dangerous	$15.00	
	978-1-944151-26-3	Street Victims	$15.00	
	978-1-944151-28-7	Street Victims II	$15.00	
	978-1-944151-30-0	Street Victims III	$15.00	
	978-1-944151-32-4	Small Wonder	$15.00	
	978-1-944151-45-4	Coup De Grace	$15.00	
	978-1-944151-47-8	Burton Boys (May 2017)	$15.00	
	978-1-944151-56-0	Burton Boys 2	$15.00	
	978-1-944151-58-4	Burton Boys 3	$15.00	
	978-1-944151-00-3	Dirty Living	$15.00	
	978-1-944151-65-2	Watch What you Say	$15.00	
		Total Books Ordered	Quantity	
			Subtotal	
	SHIPPING/HANDLING (Via U.S. Priority Mail) $7.20 for 1st book, $2.00 for each additional book Institutional Check & Money Order (No Personal Check Accepted)		Shipping	
			Total	
			Total	$

Street Knowledge Publishing LLC
1902-B Maryland Ave
Wilmington, DE 19805
TOLL FREE: 1.888.401.1114
www.streetknowledgepublishing.com

Date: _____

Purchaser _____

Mailing Address _____

City _____ State _____ Zip Code _____

Qty.	ISB Number	Title of Book	Author	Price Each	Total
	Butterfly Collection				
		Beautiful Demise	K.D Harris	$12.99	
		Scarred	K.D Harris	$12.99	
		Pressure (Coming April 2017)	K.D Harris	$12.99	
		Dying to Fit In (Coming June 2017)	K.D Harris	$12.99	
		Legacy (Coming August 2017)	K.D Harris	$12.99	
		Classy Clique (Coming Sept. 2017)	K.D Harris	$12.99	
		Caged Secrets (Coming Nov. 2017)	K.D Harris	$12.99	
		Messy Media (Coming Dec. 2017)	K.D Harris	$12.99	
	SKP Erotica				
		Beyond Measure	K.D Harris	$15.00	
		Beyond Measure II	K.D Harris	$15.00	
	978-1-944151-62-1	Beyond Measure III (April 2017)	K.D Harris	$15.00	
		The Games We Play	K.D Harris	$15.00	
		For The Love of It	K.D Harris	$15.00	
	Eric B Crime Novels				
		That Was Dirty	Wasiim	$15.00	
		It Get's Dirty	Wasiim	$15.00	
		When it Hits the Fan	Wasiim	$15.00	
		Money and Murder	Fred Brown	$15.00	
		Money and Murder II	Fred Brown	$15.00	
		Money and Murder III	Fred Brown	$15.00	
		Scandalous Ties	Jermaine "Ski" Buchanan	$15.00	
	978-1944151-51-5	Scandalous Ties II	Jermaine "Ski" Buchanan	$15.00	
	978-1-944151-52-2	Scandalous Ties III	Jermaine "Ski" Buchanan	$15.00	
	978-1-944151-55-3	Scandalous Ties IV	Jermaine "Ski" Buchanan	$15.00	
		Court in the Streets	Kevin Bullock	$15.00	
		Court in the Streets II	Kevin Bullock	$15.00	
		Court in the Streets III	Kevin Bullock	$15.00	
		Total Books Ordered	Quantity		
			Subtotal		
	SHIPPING/HANDLING (Via U.S. Priority Mail)				
	$7.20 for 1st book, $2.00 for each additional book		Shipping		
	Institutional Check & Money Order				
	(No Personal Check Accepted)		Total		
		Total	$		